contemporary romance

DANCE
IN MY
HEART

A Native American Western Novella

Marjorie Jones

CONTEMPORARY ROMANCE
Dance In My Heart
A NATIVE AMERICAN WESTERN NOVELLA

by Marjorie Jones

Indie Artist Press

~*~

Cover Art: Indie Artist Press
Published by Indie Artist Press
Eagle Mountain, Utah
www.indieartistpress.com
Large Print Edition
Copyright © 2006-2015 – All Rights Reserved
ISBN-13: 978-1-62522-034-9
April 2015

For Mom

Chapter One

The clatter of keyboards clicked through the immense newsroom, adding to Candice Lincoln's frustration as she struggled to see through the fluorescent glare obscuring her monitor. The article she labored to complete included a five o'clock deadline, and she heaved a sigh, checking the time on her Rolex.

Four-twenty-seven.

Inhaling a deep breath, she blew the air out toward her long bangs. She rolled her eyes as the blond hair fell immediately back to rest in front of them. Frustrated, she ran her manicured nails through her hair, fisting the wayward strands on the crown of her head.

"Easy, Tiger-lady," Justin Moriarty's voice brought her around in her cheap fabric swivel chair. "What's the problem?"

Releasing her hair, she picked up a sheaf of papers in both hands and shook them. "This! This is the problem. I have to compile the most worthless set of statistics, about cotton candy of all things, into an article people will actually read!"

Tossing the papers across her dull gray laminate workstation, she threw her weight into the back of her chair and propped one Gucci clad foot on the edge of her desk.

"Cotton candy?" Justin's eyebrow raised in bewilderment. "What happened to Afghanistan?"

Candice released an unladylike snort. "Why don't you ask the dragon," she replied, using her own nick-name for their senior creative director.

"Uh-oh," Justin made himself comfortable, leaning against the thin portable wall of her cubicle. "What did you do now?"

"Me? I didn't do anything. That man hates women. He despises the fact that I've managed to chase stories to the four corners of the globe, while he's been stuck in some office, reading what others have done. The fact I'm a woman and can write circles around his fat ass drives him insane."

"So you get the human interest stuff, while I, on the other hand, have just picked up plane tickets to Kuwait from purchasing?"

She sat up straight in her chair, ignoring the thud of her boot on the worn industrial carpeting. "No!"

Justin smirked. "Enjoy the candy, Candy," he laughed. "I'll send you a post card from Baghdad."

"You jerk," she threw her mechanical pencil at his chest. He caught it and after checking the lead, slipped it into his pocket.

"I know. Ain't it cool. I wonder what they're wearing in Baghdad this time of year. Sand cammo?"

"Shut up. I have work to do," she smiled. She didn't really begrudge Justin his luck. Talented and bold, and male, it was only natural he would get the in-country assignments. "And don't call me 'Candy', you know I hate that."

"Don't sweat it, babe. If anyone can make an article about spun sugar spin, you can."

She appreciated his words of encouragement, even as she doubted them. Waving him away, she resumed typing. Her bangs fell into her eyes again. Huffing, she gave up and reached for the NY Giants ball-cap hanging on a plastic hook near her computer and shoved her hair into it. She ignored the fact it added nothing to her chartreuse Armani pant suit.

Twenty minutes later, she printed the two thousand-word side-bar she'd been assigned and groaned. She missed the action of real news. If she had half a brain in her head, she'd leave NATIONAL PULSE magazine behind and write freelance. She stacked the double-spaced papers neatly and clipped them together.

Rising, she walked with a shadow of her former aplomb to the Dragon's office. Her temper threatened to flare with each step she took. She hadn't even been given the main assignment, to cover the largest ever sea-farer's festival to ever hit the New York waterways. She'd been assigned instead a worthless side-bar to investigate the intricacies of festival cousine. By the time she reached the very solid wood door of Mark Barlow's office, her level of anxiety had reached its zenith. If he said just one thing about her article, made one red mark on the pristine white paper before she left his company, she'd likely kill him.

"Come in," he called in reply to her forceful knock.

She pushed the door open and crossed the plush carpet with three long strides. Tossing the papers on the desk, she noted the time again.

"There. Eight minutes to spare." She turned to leave.

"I knew you could do it, cupcake."

A low growl clawed its way up her throat at the diminutive. She couldn't kill him, she hesitated in mid-step. She needed the paycheck.

Alimony is a bitch. Especially when her ex received it, instead of paying it. The divorce court hadn't cared she had breasts. The irony nearly made her laugh. Instead, she traced her steps back to the door.

"I have another assignment for you," he called after her.

She turned as she reached for the doorknob. "Let me guess. You want me to survey pigeons in Central Park. Find out the motivation for shitting on the statues?"

He apparently ignored her sarcasm. She knew he heard her, unless he was losing his hearing along with his hair.

"You're flying to Minnesota tomorrow morning. I want pictures and a human interest piece on the Ojibwe Indians. The dancers, specifically. They are having some kind of Pow Wow thing this weekend. You can pick up your plane tickets in purchasing."

Stunned, Candice gripped the doorknob until she thought her fingers would burst. "You didn't even check with me first? I don't want this assignment, Mark. You know how much I hate this stuff. Who gives a shit about a bunch of Indians stomping around a camp-fire! Justin is going to Kuwait. I can tag along as his photographer. I won't even have to write anything." She hated the whine sounding through her voice. She hated begging.

But Minnesota? He had to be kidding.

"No, cupcake. It's all been arranged. You're going to Minnesota, and you're going to bring back heartwarming pictures of Native Americans doing what Native Americans do. Beating drums and dancing."

She narrowed her eyes, but grit her teeth. She needed the paycheck. The words were becoming a mantra, and she hated it.

She spun out of the office and would have slammed the door behind her if the damn plush-pile carpeting weren't so thick the door barely moved at all.

She marched to her desk, picked up her Gucci bag, her Nikon, her laptop encased snugly in its leather case and raced toward the door. She needed to get out of here. Maybe she'd stop by Manny's for a drink on the way home.

No. Too many memories, she sighed as she pressed the down button on the elevator. And too many fellow reporters who still had careers. The last thing she needed right now was the off-chance of running into one of her old colleagues, all too eager to espouse their latest middle eastern jaunt.

"Nice hat, Candice," Emily Parker called from her cubicle.

She reached up and grunted as she pulled the Giant's cap from her hair. "Here, keep it," she tossed it at Emily as the elevator doors parted with a loud chime.

"Thanks."

Once on the city streets, she felt herself relax. The steamy grime of New York pumped through her veins as she made her way to the Taxi stand in front of the Time Warner Building. Horns blared, voices merged together in a cacophony of verbal music and even the screaming of the pigeons as she scattered them with her steps soothed her.

She found a cab with no trouble and situated herself in the back seat.

Pulling out her cell-phone, she gave the driver her address. Please be home, Lynette. She answered on the third ring.

"Yeah, whatcha need?"

"You're cheerful," Candice laughed. "What's up?"

"Nothing. The damn super said he'd be here by five to fix the drain in the bathroom, but he's nowhere in sight. Guess we're using Justin's shower again tonight."

"That shouldn't be a problem. He's going to Kuwait in the morning. I'm sure he'll trade running water for tending his houseplants again."

"He got the Kuwait thing? Gee, hon, I'm sorry."

Lynette Sinclair had been her roommate since college. Except for those misguided four years Candice actually tried to share her life with a man. Candice knew the sympathy she offered was genuine, and it warmed her.

"Yeah, he got it. But I didn't really expect to, you know?"

"I know. Are you on your way home?"

"Yep. In the cab as we speak."

"Did you get the candy article finished on time?"

"I did."

"Good. Call in sick tomorrow and we can take the weekend at my mom's place in Jersey. You need a break."

Candice sighed. She loved going to Lynette's mom's beach house. "I wish I could, but I'm flying to Minnesota in the morning. Damn," she cursed. "I forgot to pick up the plane ticket. This day just keeps getting better and better."

"Minnesota? What's in Minnesota?"

"I'll explain later. I'm gonna try and catch Justin to see if he'll get my stuff for me. I'll see you at home."

She hung up and dialed Justin's cell number. She caught him right as he was leaving the building, but he agreed to collect her plane ticket and car rental reservation.

"Thanks, bud. I appreciate it. Oh, and can Lynette and I use your shower again? The super is a no show."

He laughed. "Sure thing, babe. You know, it's a good thing you have me for a neighbor. Most New Yorkers would just let you stink."

"Nice image," she laughed as the cab pulled to a stop in front of her building.

Lynette met her at the door with a

cocktail and a plate of spaghetti. Ignoring the food, Candice took the drink and collapsed the minute she found the leather sofa in the tidy living room.

"So what's in Minnesota?" Lynette asked as she reclined on the other end of the couch.

"Indians, apparently."

"Oh my. You know what you need?"

Candice took a sip of her gin and tonic and swallowed. "What?"

"Really good sex with a way buff brave," Lynette answered, wiggling her eyebrows.

Candice nearly choked. "Like that would ever happen."

"No really, it would do you a world of good."

Candice tried to recall the last time

she'd had really good sex with anyone and frowned when she drew a complete blank.

Lynette kicked her gently. "Lighten up. It can only get better from here."

"Right," she drolled as she tossed back the last of her gin. She stood and grabbed the key to Justin's apartment from the hook by the kitchen pass-through. "I'm heading to J's for a shower. Back in a few."

Justin's bathroom oozed masculinity. The dark red walls, almost maroon, boasted gold accessories, including a towel warmer. She reached for the thick bronze-colored towel she'd placed there before she'd stepped into to the black marble shower and wrapped it around her dripping body.

"I thought I'd find you here," Justin

stated from the doorway.

"Shit, you scared me." She laughed and finished tucking the towel around into her cleavage.

He shook his head and winced. "Damn woman. You have a body to make a guy straight, you know that?"

"Like you would ever notice," she reached for another towel and rubbed her hair brusquely.

"Oh, I notice. I'm just not interested." He turned and headed to the dry bar in his bedroom. "You need a pick-me-up?"

"No thanks. But I do have a favor?"

"Anything, babe. Shoot."

She hedged for a minute, not sure if she should broach what could be a touchy subject. "Can I borrow some of Ray's things for my trip?"

"Sure. I moved everything into the guest room last week." He returned to the bathroom door with a large drink in his hand. "Wouldn't want any of my dates to see women's clothing in my room. They might thing a girl lives here."

"Oh, the horror," she laughed at his mock shutter. "If I remember right, didn't he have a little cowgirl get-up? I just need those boots he used to wear. I don't think my spiked Gucci's will do the trick in cowboy country."

"Sure. I'll get them for you. But I thought you were on the side of the Indians. Maybe you need moccasins."

Cowboys. Indians. Ugh.

"If I have to go," she grimaced as she pulled a brush through her hair. "I'm going cowgirl."

Chapter Two

The even rhythm of the drums reverberated in Candice's blood, keeping time with her pulse as she watched the talented musicians play. Several men, both young and old, formed a circle in a grassy clearing, surrounded by a myriad of onlookers.

When she'd arrived at the Pow Wow, held out of doors in a large state park with a huge lake shimmering in the

Saturday afternoon sun, she had been concerned about what to expect. She had no idea an event like this would bring so many segments of the population. Families out for an afternoon of fun and sun, people obviously on dates, and of course, Indians as far as she could see. She'd snapped several great photos already, but made her way now to the drummers to await the arrival of the hoop dancers.

She'd missed Friday's performance because her rental car hadn't been ready in time, but she still had ample opportunity to photograph today's show. She positioned herself near the circle and checked her film supply.

Several young girls, all of them Indian, pushed their way in front of her.

The tallest one, maybe thirteen

years old, clapped her hands anxiously. "I hope he's here. Omigod, did you see him yesterday?"

"Eya'," squealed her companions.

"And the way he moves," one girl continued, "should be against the law. You should have seen him."

"Eya'. Bishigwaadizi," the third girl added in her native language.

Candice smiled. She had no idea what the girl had said, but she received a round of blushing giggles for the comment. Apparently teenage girls were teenage girls, no matter where they lived.

The beat of the drums changed, drawing her attention to the ringed stage. Four men, dressed in native attire, including leather moccasins and what could only be eagle feathers in their long black hair danced into the circle.

Their magnificent costumes consisted of loose fitting tunics over pants in bright yellow, vibrant purple, blue and green. Intricate beadwork designs graced nearly every surface and feathers from a bird she couldn't name added a mystical softness to the image, without detracting in the least from the maleness of the scene.

One at a time, they performed fluid, apparently spontaneous movements, using multiple hoops to create patterns and shapes. Snapping photographs wildly, Candice found she really enjoyed the solemnity of the dance.

"He's not there," pouted the tall girl again. "Man, you guys said he danced in this group."

"He does, he does. He comes out later, because he's the best of them all."

As if prophesized by the girls words, he appeared. Long black hair, dressed with leather strips wrapped tightly around several strands by his temples and rich brown feathers, cascaded down his bare back. When he spun in a tight circle, the panels over his buckskin breeches flew outward, revealing his thickly muscled legs encased in the tight leather. Shirtless, he wore some kind of breastplate over his chest, but it did nothing to obscure the heavily defined muscles. His arms bulged with power as he held the hoops in strong hands, forming intricate patterns. Candice's cheeks heated as she wondered what else he could do with the trained dexterity of those fingers.

The graceful sensuality of his presence commanded wanton attention.

He moved as if he were part of the hoops, his feet flying expertly in time to the powerful drum beats.

Graceful.

Fluid.

"Omigod, he is so gorgeous," squealed the girls.

Suddenly remembering where she was and why she was there, Candice started taking photos like crazy. His face loved the camera. A strong jaw line beneath full lips and a straight nose boasted power and maleness. She pointed the camera and zoomed in on his narrowed brow as he danced. The look of concentration spoke of dedication and a love of his craft. But nothing could have prepared her for the shock of heat she experienced when he turned his nearly black eyes directly on her.

"Omigod, he's looking at us!" The girls in front of her swooned.

No. He looked directly into the lens of Candice's camera. She swallowed past the lump forming in her throat as she refocused the camera and snapped even more photos.

"Damn," she whispered as the film ran out. She lowered the camera as it automatically rewound the roll of film. She dug into her satchel for a new roll. Her fingers felt like gel as she searched blindly, unwilling to remove her eyes from him long enough to search her bag.

Was that a grin creasing his full mouth? She thought she'd seem him smile at her, and whether he did or not, she smiled in return.

The drum beats came to a sudden stop and the audience erupted into a mass of applause. The moment the dancers exited through a gate on the eastern edge of the circle, the girls in front of her rushed around the ring and accosted the poor man, as did spectators from every part of the circle. Within minutes of the last drum beat, he disappeared into a mass of fans.

She backed away and changed the film in her camera. Disappointed she hadn't snapped more pictures of him, she decided to track him down. She shook her head and laughed. After his mob had dispersed.

▲▼▲▼▲

Hawk watched the blond woman back away from the crowd. Her fingers trembled as she removed one roll of film from her expensive-looking camera and replaced it with a new one. Her body swayed slightly in the afternoon breeze and she reminded him suddenly of a reed twisting in the wind.

Long blond hair framed a delicate face and eyes the clearest shade of blue he'd ever seen rested in an inquisitive expression. Her skin glowed white, but not just like a white person. Like cream.

As if the sun refused to kiss her.

Dressed like a city-dweller would dress if they lived in the country, she definitely appeared out of her element. Skin tight Wranglers accentuated her full hips. Hips made for a man's hands. A sleeveless Wrangler shirt, pink with a yellow collar, stretched tightly across rounded breasts. Breasts made for a man's lips. He kept his eyes trained on her until the crowd of well wishers and boy-crazy girls demanded his full attention. He'd find her later.

And if the sun refused to kiss her, he would happily take up the slack.

After spending a few minutes with some of the mooning girls he always dealt with when he performed, he extricated himself to search for the yellow-haired photographer. He found her a few minutes later, seemingly waiting for someone. He experienced a twinge of unexplainable jealously as he scanned the immediate area for any male who might be her escort. He didn't see anyone, and deciding to risk it, he walked over to her.

"Anii aninishina, ozawahn weenessisee." He liked the way her breath caught in her chest when she smiled at him.

"Hello," she replied, more than likely not even realizing he'd said basically the same thing to her. She cleared her throat before speaking again. He made her nervous, he could tell.

"I'm Candice Lincoln, from *National Pulse Magazine*," she began. "I'm doing a piece on hoop dancing. I was actually hoping to meet you. I hope you don't mind that I took some pictures of you."

Time to have a little fun. He schooled his features into a frown and shook his head. "I'm sorry. I came over to take your film. I'm afraid I can't allow you to take my photograph."

He stifled a smile as she blanched. Her eyes widened as she gasped. "Oh, I'm sorry. It's a religious thing, isn't it?

You think your soul has been captured."

He couldn't do it. The look on her face stole his breath and tormenting her further would certainly damn his soul, anyway. He chuckled. "No. I'm just playing with you. Take all the photos you like. He offered his hand as he continued, "I'm called Hawk. Nice to meet you, Candice Lincoln."

Her warm fingers slipped into his and he felt her slight tremor. "So, why were you hoping to meet me?"

"I wanted to ask you some questions, if it's okay. I'm not real familiar with Indian culture," she replied.

"Native American culture isn't something you can understand in a day, Miss Lincoln. It takes dedication, and living the culture, to even begin to learn it. I've been studying my whole life, and I still learn things from the dadibaajimoowinini every time I speak with one."

"Dadibaa...," she laughed self-consciously. "I'm sorry. What does that mean?"

He liked her laugh. The sound came from inside her, with nothing even remotely like a giggle. Even with the timid lilt in her voice, he knew she possessed a confidence only few women were lucky enough to find.

"Loosely translated, it means 'storyteller'. Every chance I get, I'll sit down with one of the elders and learn a little more of our history."

"I see."

"So where do you want to start?"

"Start what?"

He laughed aloud. "Your

interview?" he reminded her.

"Oh, right," she answered, rolling her eyes. "I have no idea."

"How about a tour of the park? If you think of any questions, just yell."

"Sounds good to me."

He offered his arm and she took it. Her soft touch on his forearm sent a fire to his loins he hadn't expected. As they strolled through the crowd, he'd never been so thankful for the breech cloth portion of his regalia in his life.

"Okay, here's a question. Those women over there," she pointed toward three women selling hand-beaded jewelry from a card table covered in black velvet. "They are called squaws, right?"

He chuckled. "Well, the one in the middle, in the blue dress? She's actually called Martha. And if you call her 'squaw' you'd better do it running, because she'll probably kick your ass."

"Why on earth would she do that?" she declared boldly, a smirk hidden beneath her mock outrage.

"Because the word 'squaw' is akin to 'whore'. What would you do?"

Heat suffused her cheeks and she looked down briefly, before meeting his eyes again. "I'm sorry. I didn't know."

"It's okay. Most gichi-mookomaanag have no idea," he offered. "And before you ask, that means, white men, or Americans."

Candice felt like a fool. She'd made more verbal blunders since she'd introduced herself to Hawk than she was comfortable with. She would have to be careful not to offend him in the future. At least she could try not to. It became increasingly difficult to concentrate as she held to the firm muscles of his arm. He escorted her though the camp, as if he were some nobleman, and she a great lady. Lynette's words came back to haunt her.

...sex with a way buff brave...

"So what about you?" She stepped around a paper plate someone had abandoned on the ground.

He stooped and picked it up, crumbled it and tossed it in the trash receptacle a few feet away. "Two points. And the crowd goes wild." He turned his attention back to her. "What about me?"

"Are you called a brave?" Her heart raced. She felt like she could pool into a puddle of goo if he would just say the word.

"You watch too many westerns,

lady." He tilted his head to look down at her, his impressive height making her head spin.

She sighed and offered a wan smile. "I suppose you're right. But you have to know, I'm a city girl. Through and through. Westerns are the closest I've ever come to anything like this."

"Well, then, you haven't seen anything, yet. In answer to your question, some men are called Warriors, but they've earned it. By serving in the military, or though some act of courage."

"And do you rank among them?"

A child with a handful of bright yellow helium balloons dashed across their path. Candice stumbled and would have fallen if Hawk hadn't used his free hand on her opposite elbow to steady her. She regained her balance and stared up at him. Instead of releasing her, he slid his right hand up her left arm as he stroked her gently with the pad of his thumb.

"No. I'm just a man. Isn't that enough?"

The insinuation in his dark eyes shook her to the soles of her borrowed boots. Enough? Hell, yes, it was enough.

Chapter Three

"So how long have you been a writer?" Hawk sat next to Candice on the soft grass beside the lake. They'd spent hours wandering the grounds and now rested beneath a shade tree, eating fry bread.

"All my life," she answered with a proud smile. "Ever since I can remember."

Blood pumped through him as his

eyes rested on her rosy lips and her long, slender neck. He wanted to taste her. He decided at that moment, he would taste her. Soon.

"Why are you looking at me like that?" she asked, her voice sounding breathless.

"I want to kiss you."

She swallowed hard and the muscles in her neck contracted slightly. He nearly groaned aloud. "So why don't you?"

She didn't have to ask him twice. He put the paper plate on the ground beside him without taking his eyes from hers. He lowered his mouth toward hers slowly, leaving her room to change her mind. But he prayed to whatever god would listen that she wouldn't. By the time he reached her lips, he thought he would die with wanting. He'd never before felt such a pull of attraction to a woman before.

He'd had flings, even one bona-fide relationship, in college. But nothing, no one, had ever tempted him like this before.

Finally, his lips met hers. He kissed her briefly, barely nipping her bottom lip with his teeth. She parted her lips and raised her face to grant him more intimate contact. This time, he did groan as he took her face in both his hands and deepened the kiss. She tasted sweet, like her name. He knew she would. Her tongue played with his as he swirled it inside her mouth in an ancient erotic rhythm. She leaned into him, her breasts brushing the breastplate of his regalia. He wanted out of it. He wanted to feel her sliding naked against him. He was no expert, but based on her reaction to his hands stroking through her hair, she wanted it too.

Could he risk it? Did he dare?

She moaned into his mouth and he knew he would.

Pulling away, he rested his forehead against hers. Through heaving breaths, he panted, "How far is your hotel?"

"Twenty minutes," she breathed. I'm parked right over there."

"I have my Indian. I'll follow you."

She smiled broadly. "Your 'Indian'?"

He laughed from somewhere deep inside, where he'd never known he existed. "Yeah, I know. Believe me, I've heard it from just about everyone already. But I didn't name the damn bike."

▲▼▲▼▲

Candice couldn't believe any of this was happening. She raced through traffic like a woman possessed, ignoring the other drivers, except the man on the bright red motorcycle directly behind her. He'd changed his clothes at the park. He went into the tipi like a man out of time, and came out wearing thigh hugging faded blue denim jeans, a white T-shirt and black leather jacket. Under one arm, he tucked a shining black helmet. He'd taken the feathers and leather out of his hair, which lifted from his shoulders as the wind kicked it.

Her sweating palms slid over the

steering wheel. She was really going to do it. Propriety be damned, she was going to ravish him. Heat pooled in her womb and throbbed through her limbs as she maneuvered her rented Corsica around a semi tractor-trailer. Nearly missing her exit, she swerved in front of the truck. The air horn reverberated around her. She laughed. She'd never been this crazy in her life. What was wrong with her?

She didn't care.

Checking the rearview mirror, she found Hawk keeping pace with her. Good. If she'd lost him, she'd just die. Her tires squealed as she made a sharp left into the parking garage of her hotel. She skidded to a halt on the first level. Hawk pulled into a space not far from hers.

"Lady, you're dangerous," he

declared as she climbed from the car.

"I can't help it. I so rarely get to drive."

"I'm not complaining."

"Good," she replied over her shoulder as she led him to the elevator.

Once inside the lift, he turned on her with ferocious passion. Pushing her against the back wall, he feasted on her lips before dropping his mouth to run his tongue over her jaw. She tilted her head back as she clung to him like a drowning victim. His body pressed against hers and she felt the hardness of his erection against her belly.

"God, you taste good," he breathed against her neck. "You're killing me."

His hair tickled her bare arms as he moved his body over hers. She arched against him, silently begging him to touch her. He read her mind as well as he read her body, she decided, as his firm grip found her breast and kneaded the flesh through her shirt and bra. Killing him? She teetered on the brink of damnation.

She moaned as his other hand cupped her behind and drew her pelvis into him. Her body reacted instantly and she nearly came undone.

The chime sounded and they jumped apart. His hair fell over his eyes slightly, but he never took those dark orbs from her. She checked the floor indicator over the doors as they opened to admit an elderly couple. Sixth Floor. Halfway home.

Hawk studied Candice's flushed cheeks and shining eyes. Her chest heaved with breathless wanting, though she tried to hide it. He chuckled as she shifted uncomfortably on her long, slim legs. His mouth watered to taste her again. If he didn't have her soon, he would burst.

The old man pushed the floor above hers.

Damn. He wouldn't be able to touch her again until they reached her room. He drew in an unsteady breath. On the opposite side of the car from her, he inhaled her scent of sex and woman. He smiled a knowing grin, and she blushed again. What were the old couple thinking? Did they know what was about to happen between the young people sharing the elevator? He caught the silent, knowing glance the old man threw him and laughed. Yeah, the old man knew exactly what was going on.

The doors opened on the twelfth floor and Candice made a move to exit. Hawk followed her lead as the old man cleared his throat. "Have fun, kids."

Candice stopped dead in her tracks, half in and half out of the car. Hawk placed his hand on the small of her back, urging her forward as he answered over his shoulder. "We will, grandfather," he laughed.

The doors closed.

"I can't believe he just said that," Candice declared, her cheeks rosy with embarrassment.

"I can. The tension in there was so thick you could cut it with a knife. They're old... not stupid."

Candice pulled a keycard from her satchel and struggled with the magnetic door lock. Pressing himself against her back, he moved her hair off her neck before cupping her waist in his hands. He nibbled on the back of her neck, until finally, the resistance in front of her subsided and the door swung open.

Without releasing her, he followed her step for step into the large suite. She dropped her camera and satchel on the floor beside the dresser and TV stand, and spun in his arms. He captured her mouth again, taking her bottom lip between his teeth and gently tugging on the full flesh. Damn. He was going to die, right here, right now, and he didn't give a flying fuck.

She kissed him back, pulling him into her before running her hands inside his open jacket and sliding it off his shoulders. He let the heavy leather fall to the floor, then scooped her off her feet and carried her to the bed. His body burned wherever she touched him, trails of fire branding him like an iron.

Laying her on the bed, he stood over her and removed his T-shirt. She smiled appreciatively as her eyes roamed over his chest then settled on his buttoned jeans. He couldn't stop the grin from escaping. She made him want to smile. Hell, she made him want to sing, for crying out loud.

She pushed herself up to her knees and slowly removed her shirt. Beneath it, a teal lace bra did little to hide her breasts from him. The dark circles of her nipples showed through the thin fabric.

"Oh, hell," he breathed. "Eya'."

He sat on the edge of the bed and leaned forward to unlace his boots. She pressed her body against him for a moment then pulled away. Where the flesh of his back had simmered for a mere moment, he now froze. His suffering lasted only a second before her naked breasts seared him. She moved his hair out of her way and trailed hot, wet kisses down his back.

He kicked his boots off and straightened. With trembling fingers he unbuttoned his jeans. When he stood to remove them, he allowed himself the luxury of turning to face her. Shock and undeniable ecstasy coursed through him. She kneeled on the bed gloriously naked. Her eyes smoldered and called to him.

The room spun, heated only by their bodies and the promise of pleasure so untamed Candice thought she might actually swoon. Like some wanton, she sat on the bed begging him silently to take her. This man she didn't even know, but whom she knew better than herself at that moment. The twilight sky filtered through the windows, shadowing the rock hard planes of his body. He lowered his jeans, kicked them absently across the floor and joined her on the bed. They remained on their knees, the heated hurried coupling replaced with tenderness as he ran the pad of his thumb over her mouth. She licked it with the tip of her tongue and watched the heat in his eyes jump a notch.

"Are you sure?" he asked her simply, his head tilted in that way he had which meant he didn't want to hurt her feelings.

"Yes," she breathed, not sure if she'd spoken aloud.

"Good."

Then he attacked with a passionate force she'd never known a man could possess. He devoured her lips, her neck. He stoked a fire within her searching limbs until the liquid heat burned a path to her most secret places. He laid her down, separating her thighs with his leg. He played with her hair, running his dexterous fingers across her scalp, and cupped her breast with the other. When his lips found her breast, his hand moved to stroke between her thighs. He slipped a strong finger inside her and she arched against it.

"Oh, god," she cried. "Don't stop."

"I won't stop, ozawahn weenessisee. Not until you beg me to."

"Never, never stop," she curled against him as he continued to delve inside of her. Almost immediately, she came apart. His touch was sheer heaven and she'd witnessed the glory first hand.

He allowed her only a moment of respite before he positioned himself between her legs. His thick shaft rested at the entrance to her soul, teasing her with promised passion. "Open your eyes, ozawahn weenessisee. Look at me."

She did as he asked and found him on the brink of losing control, if the crease in his brow were any indication. She'd never felt beautiful before. She'd never considered herself in the same vein as those women who could drive a man to distraction. But she felt beautiful now. He made her feel like the most desirable woman in the world.

"I want to see your eyes when I take you."

Then he did. With all the graceful

flight of his namesake, he brought her to heights of passion she'd never known existed.

Chapter Four

Hawk removed the spent condom and made sure it landed in the lined garbage can in the bathroom. He grinned as he remembered the expression on Candice's face when he'd taken off the first one.

"Where did that come from?" she'd laughed.

"It's all in the timing," he'd replied. And it was. In the few moments she'd spent descending from her first of many orgasms, he'd slipped it on.

As often as he preached to the kids on the res about safe sex, he couldn't very well break his own rules.

He made his way back to the bed, where Candice lay in naked splendor, her lips swollen from his kisses. She finished a strawberry dipped in whipped cream and he grinned lazily at her. The things she could do with that tongue drove him mad with desire. Just thinking about it made his shaft twitch.

"Come back to bed," she purred.

"We're out of ummm... supplies, ozawahn weenessisee. If I come back to bed, it'll be to sleep," he replied, shaking his head. "Unfortunately."

He knew he could easily go again, even though he'd just tossed the last of a six-pack of Trojans into the wastebasket. She fueled him like no other woman ever had. Addictive, he couldn't get enough of her.

"Come to bed anyway. It's late."

He slid between the sheets and she leaned into his chest. He ran a tendril of her hair through his fingers, until he finally lifted a thick strand to his nose and inhaled deeply her lush scent.

Amazing woman.

"So you're the safe-sex guru, I guess," she teased lightly as she found an empty condom wrapper among the sheets and set it on the bedside table.

"I just like to set a good example. Too many kids having kids these days. The Native American population is no different. Maybe even worse."

"How so?" The compassion in her

voice sounded genuine, and he lifted his head slightly to see her narrowed brows.

"I guess when a person feels like no one cares, they'll search for love anywhere they can find it."

"I suppose," she whispered. The vague tone in her voice unsettled him. Was that what she was doing? He found it hard to believe a woman like her had trouble feeling loved. She probably had a boyfriend or husband back home, and he satisfied her urge to walk on the wild side. Lots of women, white women, came on to him for just that reason. For some reason he couldn't place, the thought she did the same annoyed him. But something in her voice settled his angst. She sounded lost, as if she reached for something she felt she could never have.

She yawned against his chest, her

warm breath teasing him awake again. How could he possibly lie here and not take her again? It seemed impossible.

"I've been meaning to ask you, Hawk. What exactly do you keep calling me?"

"Wanton. Beautiful. Vixen." He lied with a lop-sided grin.

She chuckled as sleep swept over her. "You called me that when we first me? Somehow, I think you're pulling my leg."

He laughed. "Yellow Hair," he confessed. "I've been calling you Yellow Hair. You have the beauty of the sun in you, Candy. I will feel its warmth for the rest of my life."

The even rhythm of her breaths told him she slept. A part of him was happy she hadn't heard his last comment. If she did search for something... No, if she searched for love, he couldn't give it to her. He was far too busy to complicate his life with a woman like her. A woman like her deserved attention, admiration, worship.

He had none of those things to give her.

▲▼▲▼▲

Candice hovered on the edge of sleep. Her body ached from the intensity of Hawk's attentions, and the unfamiliar mattress. As memories of the night before slid through her consciousness, her belly tightened. Reaching her arm over toward him, she grinned like the proverbial Cheshire cat.

Her smile faded as her searching

fingers met cold sheets. She opened her eyes to find Hawk's pillow empty. She sat up and scanned the hotel room. No jacket on the floor where she'd dropped it. No jeans against the far wall. No motorcycle helmet in sight.

"Hawk?" she called. Was he in the bathroom?

No deep timbered voice answered her.

What had she expected? Flowers? Harps? The heavens to open and rain perpetual love and commitment on her shoulders? She didn't want any of that. She may be dissatisfied with her job at the moment, but she definitely liked most of her life exactly the way it was. She'd known going into it last night this was a one night stand. By Monday, she'd be on a plane home. Back to her real life, with some pretty amazing, gut-clenching memories.

She threw back the covers and made her way to the shower. By the time she finished, she'd come to terms with what she'd done.

"Just don't make it a habit, little girl," she censured herself.

The phone rang and she dashed pick it up. Maybe it was Hawk?

She shook her head and dismissed the thought.

"Yeah, Lincoln here."

"What are you doing?"

Great. The dragon, himself. "It's Sunday morning, Mark. What do you think I'm doing? I'm recovering from a sex marathon with a tribal dancer."

"Very funny," came his humorless reply. He thought she was kidding. She nearly laughed aloud. "Listen, I've changed your flight to Wednesday. I need you to visit the reservation and get some more history on the tribe."

She rolled her eyes. "I haven't even submitted the story yet, Mark."

"I know. And I'm sure what you have is fine, but we lost a story and I need to fill the space. Go find out what you can about the history of the dance, where Joe Blow City can take lessons, that sort of thing."

She heaved a sigh. Man, he irritated her. First, he shoved this piece down her throat, now he expected her to drag it out.

Still, she couldn't be sorry. Not after her night with Hawk. "Fine. I'll head out there Monday morning. See what I can dig up."

"Good girl, cupcake. I knew I could

count on you."

She hung up without saying good-bye. Cupcakes can't talk. She stuck her tongue out at the phone and got dressed.

The day seemed to loom before her, empty and long. She tried to write an opening to her story, but found her eyes falling on her camera and satchel repeatedly. She could find a photo supply shop and develop her pictures. She returned her eyes to the blank screen on her laptop. Sure was a better idea than sitting her making herself crazy.

An hour and a half later, she screwed a red bulb into the hotel room bathroom light fixture. Her credit card weighed a few dollars more, but soon she'd be developing her film and looking into the image of dark eyes and smooth, muscled flesh.

She felt the heat in her cheeks and the clenching in her belly at the mere thought of Hawk. She smiled like a fool. Hopeless. Yep. That's her.

Another hour passed before she hung the last of the first roll of film on the strings she'd mounted across her hotel room. She liked the black and whites the best, she decided. While the color shots were more detailed, the black and whites offered insight into the spirit of his movements. Just like him, they pretended to be out of some past time and place.

She walked the length of the string, examining each photograph. As she did so, a tremor moved up her spine as if he still touched her.

She nearly giggled at the warm sensations heating her blood. She felt sixteen again. Taking down a nearly dried photograph, she traced the plane of his rigid stomach, her finger hovering just above the surface of the print.

She didn't know his full name.

The realization brought with it a void in the memories she had of him. Somehow, it didn't seem right that she shouldn't know him more. On the other hand, she knew everything she needed to know.

She'd never see him again.

Chapter Five

The road loomed empty before her as Candice consulted her map for the third time to verify she traveled the correct road. She swerved enough to scare herself, and corrected her direction before putting the map aside. She'd driven nearly half a day, and if she didn't find the Ojibwe reservation soon, she would be forced to turn back.

A battered sign with bright red and

yellow paint peeling from sun and water damaged boards approached on the right side of the car. "Welcome to Cedar Lake Summit U.S. Government Ojibwe Resettlement Camp."

She glanced around her. Nothing but grasslands as far as she could see. But satisfied she was at least heading in the right direction, she kept driving. A few minutes later, she pulled into a small market. The windows gleamed in the early afternoon light, even though the paint on the old clapboard building showed signs of wear.

An elderly man sat in a misplaced restaurant booth set awkwardly outside the front door. He dragged on his pipe and tilted up his straw cowboy hat slightly at her arrival.

Stepping from the car, she smiled at

him. "Hello. Can you tell me if there is an office or where I can talk to someone in charge of the reservation?" she asked.

He stared back at her without speaking. Either he didn't understand her, or he couldn't hear her, she decided finally, and continued into the store.

"Anii aninishina," a young Native American woman called from behind a scarred laminate counter. "What can I do for you today?"

Candice walked to the counter and took off her sunglasses. "I'm wondering if there is a central office here on the reservation, or where I might find someone who can answer a few questions about hoop dancing?"

"You a reporter?"

She smiled. "Yes, how did you know?"

"White people only come here for two reasons. One is to bring us charity, you know books, blankets, things like that. Like we don't have our own blankets," she rolled her eyes. "The rest are reporters. You don't have a bus of kids and a truck full of blankets, so you're a reporter."

"Well, you're right. So who should I talk to?"

"Michael Manone works in the main building. It's a red brick job about six miles up the way you're going. He can probably point you in the right direction. And he's sort of like a manager. Takes care of lots of things for lots of people."

"Michael Manone, got it. Thanks a lot," she turned to leave.

The woman's voice brought her back around. "You're going to right a nice article, aren't you?"

"A nice article?" she felt her confusion play across her features.

"Yeah. You're not going to make us sound like were worthless and can't do anything right, are you? Because if that's the case, you can get back into your fancy car and drive straight back to your side of the line."

"I'm writing about the beauty and magic of hoop dancing," she stated slowly, hoping she expressed the sincerity she felt.

The woman smiled. "Good. Then welcome. Mike should be able to help you out."

It didn't take her long to find the main building. A low brick structure with few windows, it reminded her of an old dentist's office. She parked in front and entered through double glass doors on the North side.

A bell sounded her entrance into the shadowed lobby. Avocado green shag carpet covered an uneven floor and appeared to have passed its prime years ago. The cheap paneling on the walls screamed nineteen-seventy-two. A older woman stood beside a desk behind a counter with cages resembling and old-western bank.

"You're going to hurt yourself. Be careful."

A muffled male voice came from out of sight behind the desk. "I know what I'm doing, Celeste."

"Just don't electrocute yourself. I'll be right back."

She came to the window and smiled at Candice. A heavy-set woman, she looked to be in her late fifties, with a small spattering of gray in her two long braids. She wore a bright red cotton dress and a necklace of multicolored beads. "Boozhoo," she sighed. "I'm sorry you had to wait. We just got a new computer this morning, and we're still setting everything up. What can I do for you?"

"I'm looking for Michael Manone. A woman at the store out by the highway said I could find him here?"

"Well, you can when he's not crawling around under my desk. I don't have an appointment listed for him. What did you need?"

"I don't have an appointment. I was hoping he could answer a few questions for me."

"Celeste, I need you to hand me those other cords," the voice from the desk boomed.

She turned and shouted back. "I'm talking with someone, Mike. Take a break and get your behind up here. She wants you." Celeste turned back to face Candice with an exasperated look on her face. "Kids. They can't do nothing for themselves these days."

The love shining in her black eyes lightened her features, despite the words. Candice felt herself smiling. Obviously, these two people shared a bond.

"I'll be right there," the voice grumbled.

Two legs encased in black denim and tipped with cowboy boots backed out from behind the desk. From her position on the opposite side of the cages, Candice had only a narrow view of the floor, but she could see Michael Manone's form scoot from behind the old office furniture. A neat pony-tail of rich black hair rested on his back. Then he stood up and faced her.

Hawk.

Candice's heart stopped beating. At least, she felt like it did. Her breath whooshed out of her chest and her pulse froze.

"Candice?" He looked uncomfortable as he hurried around two unoccupied desks and opened a swinging door in the counter. He stopped several feet from her in the lobby. "What are you doing here? How did you..."

"I had no idea I'd find you here," she cut him off. Well, at least now she knew exactly where she stood with him. If Saturday night had meant nothing to him, she certainly didn't need him thinking she'd tracked him down for happily-ever-after time. "I'm working. My editor wanted me to find out some history and background on hoop dancing, and since I neglected to gather the information... before... I thought this would be a good place to start."

"You two know each other?" Celeste asked.

"We met at the Pow Wow," he answered Celeste a little too swiftly. What did he think? That she would go into some sordid Penthouse explanation of their relationship?

"I'm a reporter," she handed Celeste her business card.

"Come on into my office. I have some books and things you can take a look at."

She followed him through the maze

of desks to a small, sparsely furnished office in the rear of the building. He offered her a chair in front of his desk, while he took the seat behind.

He never once met her eyes. Instead, he rummaged through a bookshelf behind his desk and brought out five worn paperback texts. "This should answer all your questions. Glance through them and I can get you photocopies of whatever parts you think might help."

She picked up the first book and ran the pages off her fingers absently. "Are you okay?"

"What?" His head snapped up and finally, she could see the dark orbs set deeply into his face. How she loved his eyes.

"I said, 'are you okay'?"

Hawk couldn't believe she sat in the chair across from his desk. He'd thought he'd never see her again. All day yesterday, her image had haunted him, shaming him for what he'd done. She deserved better.

And now she wanted to know if he was okay? If he was okay? He'd treated her badly, running out in the middle of the night like a boy afraid of himself. Well, not the middle of the night. They'd spent the middle of the night exploring each other's bodies and learning the intimate desires they shared. He'd left at dawn. As she slept soundly against him in the early morning rays of the run, he'd slipped from under her relaxed cheek and arms, and left without even waking her.

He heaved a sigh. He should be shot. "No, I'm not."

She tilted her head, sending cascades of yellow curls over her shoulder. "No?"

He shook his head. "No. I owe you an apology."

"You do?"

"Eya'. Yes, I do. For the way I left. That was... wrong."

"Oh." Her brows came together as if he'd confused her. "What should you have done?"

Stunned by her question, he thought for a moment. "Said goodbye?"

She set the book down on the desk and leaned back in the chair. "Listen, Hawk. We had a good time. I'm a big girl and I can take care of myself. If I'd had half my wits about me, I would have taken care of these details that night, and you'd never have to see me again."

Except every night when he closed his eyes.

"Then you don't hate me?"

She waved her slender hand and smiled, but it didn't reach her eyes. "Of course not. How could I possibly hate Mr. Stud?"

He studied her. Regardless of her relaxed posture, her structured movements and her words, he saw her pain reflected in the watered blue of her eyes. No, he'd hurt her. What good would come from calling her bluff? Nothing, he decided, so he let her have her way.

Celeste came into the office, just in time to break the tension. He breathed a little easier. "I'm sorry to interrupt, but there are three boys out front who need to talk to you. It sounds important. One of them is Jeremy Littlefeather."

"I'm sorry, Candy. I have to see them. Have you had lunch yet?"

"No," she replied.

Against his better judgment, he continued, "Why don't you wait outside and when I'm finished with the kids, I'll take you to a little place I know in town."

"Sure," she answered with a hint of hesitation.

He stood and walked her to the door. Her eyes fell on the gold nameplate glued to the wood.

"Michael Irontree. Tribal Social Worker," she read aloud. "That's you?"

"Eya'. Manone means Irontree. Actually it means Ironwood Tree, but the university I attended screwed it up, and it stuck."

She scanned him from his eyes, to

his boots and back again. He felt the blood rush to his loins and settle there with passionate vengeance. "It fits."

Chapter Six

Hawk seated Candice at a small table in the center of the crowded diner, then took the seat opposite for himself and grabbed the menu. He'd spent nearly an hour with the three boys who came to see him while she perused the hoop dancing books he'd loaned her.

He still felt tense. He admitted to himself it wasn't his guilt alone which made him stiff with tension. He still wanted her. Were they alone right now, he would take on the tabletop. He really should be taken out and shot.

"Thank you for the books," she offered.

"No problem."

"You're not still upset about this weekend, are you?"

"Who me? Nah. I'm a rock."

She laughed. "Good. Because you didn't offend me in the least. I know how these things work."

How these things work? He hated her thinking of him like that. He'd never had a one-night stand in his life. Not that he hadn't had the opportunity, but he was raised better than that. Women were something to be treasured, not used. And he'd used her. Given the chance, he couldn't swear he wouldn't do it again.

The light, spilling from the picture windows behind her, cast a halo effect around her golden hair. She looked like an angel and he'd treated her like a whore.

"So what's good here?"

He cleared his throat before answering and shifted his position in the chair. His entire body ached to hold her, one very specific aching part of his body wanted to do more than that. "The turkey club, or if you have a real appetite, the chili burger is good too."

"Hey girly, whatcha doing here with Tonto. You his parole officer?"

Hawk's body tensed for a whole new reason at the slur. He fisted his hands, nearly ripping the menu he held in his white knuckled grip.

To her credit, Candice ignored the

remarks and continued to scan her own menu.

"Hey, I'm talking to you!"

Hawk sensed her lack of comfort. She had no idea what to do, he reckoned. She'd probably never been faced with this sort of blatant racism in her whole, sheltered, white existence.

"Just ignore him. That's Wiley Cotton. He's an asshole."

She swallowed, and replied with a barely perceptible nod. "We can go somewhere else?"

"I don't run from assholes."

She leveled her gaze on him and he felt the impact of her eyes to his core. "But it bothers you."

It wasn't a question. How did she see inside him like that? The connection they shared unnerved him, but he couldn't lie. "Eya'. Yes, it bothers me."

The waitress stopped by Wiley's table before she came to take their order. "I'm sorry about that Mike. You want me to give him the boot?"

"No, Leslie. It's okay. I wouldn't want to cost you your tip," he smiled at the woman he'd known since high school. "I'll have a chili burger and a Coors. And for the lady?" He looked at Candice and noticed her eyes misted as she studied the menu like it was the missing Dead Sea Scroll.

"A salad," she completed for him, her voice hoarse. "And a Diet Coke with lemon?"

"Sure thing, hon. Dressing?"

"Vinegar and oil, please."

When she handed the menu to Leslie, the laminated card-stock shook wildly. Candice put her hands in her lap and glanced at him. "I'm sorry. I'm being silly."

"No, you're not. But don't worry about it. His bark is worse than his bite."

"How do you put up with something like that? I mean, I've covered stories from Moscow to the Middle East, and I've never seen anything so vicious."

"You've been lucky. This is nothing, Candy. Really. Ignore him."

"You must be the most laid back guy I've ever met. Does nothing rile you?"

"Sure. Lots of things."

Men who take advantage of lonely woman and skulk off into the night without so much as the proverbial 'thank-you ma'am', for instance.

"Like what?"

"Let's see. This week, it's the unemployment rate on the res. We're up to eighty-nine point four percent this month. And then there's the teen pregnancy rate. That's down to eighty-four percent. I'm saving my temper-tantrum about alcoholism until next month."

"Is it that bad?"

Their drinks arrived and she took the wrapper off her straw. She used the straw to sink the lemon wedge in her coke before she took a sip.

"It's getting better," he shrugged. "This is the seventh generation. A time for change and prosperity. The new kids, the one's coming up now, are smarter than their parents and grandparents. I'm hoping within a few years, things will really start to change."

"So what exactly do you do?"

"Like the fake gold plastic on the door said. I'm a social worker."

"Okay, so you take children away from their parents and you're the safe-sex poster child."

Her reminder of their liaison sent a tremble down his spine. He did his best to ignore the continued pulsing in his groin. "I don't take children from their parents unless I have to. Most of the time, we can change a few habits and return the child to her home. But sometimes, yeah. Sometimes, just like in the rest of the world, the child is placed permanently. Mostly, I co-ordinate youth activities, sponsor education workshops, counsel the kids and their parents. That sort of thing."

"What kind of activities?"

Leslie placed a large salad in front of Candice. He shifted his weight back and took his elbows off the table so she could set his chili burger in front of him. He lifted the top bun and removed most of the chili before he replaced it and took a bite.

"Lots of things. Last month, we took the youth group rock-climbing. The month before, we went to the Mall of the Americas."

"That sounds like fun."

"I guess so."

"It wasn't?"

He suddenly wished he hadn't brought it up. Two of his female teen-age charges had been caught up in a scuffle at the movie theater and suffered more taunting insults than Wiley's limited brain could ever come up with. The girls had cried nearly the whole trip home. He'd done his best to console them, but he couldn't take the burning impression of the local boys' hands off of them. Where did these kids learn this shit? Sexual assault at the age of fifteen was inexcusable.

"No. It was great," he lied. He'd already shattered Candice's illusions more than enough for one afternoon. She didn't need to hear about something this dirty.

"You're lying, but that's okay. You don't have to tell me."

He looked into her eyes. He still couldn't figure out how she knew so much of him. But then, he'd always been a lousy liar.

They finished the remainder of the meal in friendly silence.

Candice pushed her nearly empty plate away, and reached for her wallet with trembling hands. Her mind whirled with the memories of his expert touch and nimble fingers. Her pulse raced in a cadence reminiscent of the drums he'd danced to on Saturday. It was as if he danced in her heart.

"Put your money away. I've got it."

He placed a twenty-dollar bill on the table and reached for her hand, apparently to help her to her feet. He threw a wave at Leslie, the waitress.

"See ya later, Mike," she called from behind the register.

"She seems nice," Candice offered. "Have you known her long?"

"Since high school."

Candice weighed the possibility that they had dated, surprised at how much she didn't appreciate the possibility. A hand reached out and held her arm, stealing her wayward thoughts back to her surroundings. She looked at the hand and followed the large arm with her eyes until she glared into the face of Wiley Cotton.

"Whatcha gonna leave with him for? You his squaw woman?"

"Let her go, Wiley," Hawk spat from her side. "Now."

Wiley's expression turned ominous, but he did release her arm. Gaining his feet, he matched Hawk's height, but his girth boasted too much beer instead of solidly packed muscle.

"It's okay, Hawk. Let's just leave." Tension grew in her belly as he watched the two men face each other, one man's expression as deadly as the other. They wouldn't fight right here in the diner. Would they?

"You better do as she says, Tonto. 'Fore you get hurt."

"Shut up, Wiley," a man shouted from the door. Candice's eyes instinctively shot in the direction of the newcomer.

A uniformed sheriff's deputy stood in silhouette as the heavy metal and glass door eased closed behind him. The deputy continued speaking as he removed a pair of wire rimmed sunglasses. "I mean it Wiley. Not another sound, or I'll take you in."

"On what charge, Carl. Speaking?"

"On whatever charge I damn well please. Now sit back down." To Candice, he said, "Miss? If you were on your way out, I suggest you continue on your way."

Candice raised her face to Hawk's, searching his eyes for his intentions. She may not know him well, but she'd been around men enough to know each one had his limit of patience. Had Hawk reached his?

"Go on. I'll be out in a minute. I'll meet you at your car."

As she stepped away from Wiley and Hawk, the deputy pushed the door open.

The diner, rife with tension, grew increasingly silent as patrons caught on to what was happening at the booth by the door.

Hawk closed his fists at his sides. Wiley Cotton was hardly worth his time or his energy. He'd never before allowed his bigotry and ignorance to get under his skin quite like this. But when he'd touched Candice, Hawk thought he would explode. He sensed Carl's slow approach and reluctantly turned his gaze to his old friend.

"Your lady friend is waiting."

The words were more than a statement. They were Carl's invitation for Hawk to leave the diner.

He would leave. He'd been on his way out anyway. He gritted his teeth and stared into Wiley's eyes as he spoke to Carl. "I'm going. But if he touches her again, I'll kill him."

He stalked out of the diner, his temper raw and callused. Where the hell had that come from? He'd just threatened a man's life in front of a law enforcement officer. That would look terrific on his resume.

Candice sat behind the wheel of her

car, cranking the engine. He slid into the seat beside her. She stopped turning the key and shifted her weight to better face him.

"You okay?"

"Yeah. I'm great. How are you?"

She smiled. He was being an ass, and he knew it. She took his tense demeanor in stride, though. Most women would tell him to shove it, but she seemed to sympathize with him. Just being this close to her made everything better.

She reached over and patted his thigh before turning the key one last time. The engine roared to life and she pointed them back to the reservation. If he had any hope of escaping the invisible net she threw to him, he needed her to leave. Soon.

Only one problem with that plan. He didn't want her to go anywhere. Except, maybe back to bed.

Chapter Seven

The drive back to the reservation seemed to take less time than when she first arrived. Candice pulled her rented Corsica into a parking space in front of Hawk's office. Her eyes fell onto the bright red Indian motorcycle parked horizontally directly beside the building. How had she missed it earlier?

It didn't matter, really. What mattered was she didn't want to say good-bye to Hawk. Her stomach clenched with remembered passion.

"Here we are." She couldn't bring herself to look at him.

"Yeah, here we are."

She reached into her satchel and removed the books. "Thanks for letting me photocopy these." She handed him the books and his hand brushed against her fingers as he took them from her. Heated shockwaves raced up her arm and settled with tingling intensity in her breasts.

Please, don't say it? Don't say good-bye.

"I'm glad I had a chance to see you again. I really am sorry about the way I left."

"I'm glad too," she whispered before clearing her throat. "And please, stop apologizing. You didn't do anything wrong."

He offered her a tentative grin. When he leaned toward her, her breath caught in her chest. Was he going to kiss her?

Please, let him kiss her. An instant later, he shoved open the car door and climbed outside. Leaning into the window, he stared into her eyes. "I'm glad I know you, ozawahn weenessisee."

She didn't have time to answer before he disappeared into his office building. Her heart shattered into pieces, searing her from the inside out. She already missed him.

The sigh trapped in her lungs finally escaped. Dwelling on the impossible would get her nowhere. She should have learned that lesson when she and her husband called it quits. She thought she had, until she met Hawk.

She turned the ignition key, telling herself things would be clearer in the morning.

The engine stuttered, then died. She pumped the gas pedal twice, then tried to turn it over again. A clicking sound echoed through the cabin. She backed off and tried again.

More clicking.

This time, the clicking slowed, until, when she tried a third time, nothing happened. No click. No roaring engine. Nothing.

Great. Now what?

She leaned her forehead on the steering wheel and glanced sideways at the red brick building.

The clock ticked time away as if nothing mattered. Maybe the clock was smarter than him, but Hawk couldn't shake the feeling he'd just thrown his whole life away. She was probably half way back to her hotel by now, he smiled ruefully. The way she drove, that might not be an exaggeration.

Actually, only ten minutes had passed since he left her in the car. He already regretted not kissing her. He wanted to taste her again. He needed it.

Unable to concentrate, he packed several files into his black leather backpack and shut down his computer.

He didn't even have a picture of her, he sighed. Damn, but he was a wimp. His own thoughts sounded like the idiotic, pubescent ramblings of his boy's group.

Get over yourself. She probably won't even remember your name next week. He threw his pack over one arm and headed out of his office.

"I wouldn't ask, but my cell phone died, and I just need to call a tow truck."

His head snapped up at the sound of Candice's voice in the lobby. His feet carried him swiftly in her direction of their own accord. She spoke with Celeste, looking a little sheepish and entirely beautiful.

"You won't get one to come out here this late. At least, not for a tow clear into the city," he answered. "What's wrong?"

"It's officially dead, I think. I'm no mechanic, but at the very least, the battery is dead, and I'm not real keen on driving half a day on borrowed power."

Were the spirits trying to tell him something? Twice now, he'd left this woman and twice she'd come back through no design of her own. If he were his brother, Adam, he'd consult the spirit world. But he wasn't a dream-walker, like his older brother. He was just a man with gut reactions. And right now his gut told him to not look a gift horse in the mouth.

"Well then, it looks like you're stuck here. I have room at my place."

Certifiably crazy. He really should seek help.

Still, he held his breath as he waited for her reply. She hesitated and then took a step in his direction. "Are you inviting me to spend the night at your house, Hawk?"

"Eya'. Yes." His heart felt like it would explode. He tried to cover his anticipation by leaning easily on the counter.

"Are you going to be there when I wake up?"

"Wild horses couldn't drag me away."

"In that case, I'd love to."

He felt like a little boy on Christmas as his mouth spread into a huge grin. He felt like dancing. "Good. Here, take this," he handed her his motorcycle helmet. I only have the one, so you better take it."

"Take it?" she quizzed him.

"Yeah. You wear it on your head," he smiled. "When you ride on a motorcycle. You know?" He hinted with a fair dose of sarcasm.

"You want me to ride on the back of

your motorcycle," she replied.

He laughed at the inflection in her half-statement, half-question. "Of course. How did you think we would get there?"

Her eyes widened for a split second before she squared her shoulders as if she prepared for battle.

"Have you never ridden on a bike before?" he hedged, taking her elbow and leading her toward the door.

"Well, sure," she cleared her throat. "I mean, the kind you pedal. The ones that go really slow and don't take high-octane."

"Well, then, Candy. You're in for a treat," he smiled as he pushed open the glass door.

The wind had picked up in the last few minutes. Dark clouds circled on the horizon. The whipping snap of the

American Flag on top of the building cracked like a bottle-rocket above their heads.

"You better grab anything you need out of your car. You can put some things in the saddlebags on my ride."

Candice had ridden in a tank once. She'd flown on a zip line in the Amazon, stood twenty feet from the edge of a live volcano and once, she'd even scuba-dived with a Great White Shark. But she'd never had the nerve to climb on the back of a motorcycle.

Insane. She thought she'd be terrified, but instead, her lips spread into a wide grin as she lifted her laptop and camera from the backseat of the car, locked the doors and pocketed the keys.

A very few minutes later, her items stowed neatly in black leather satchels covered in silver tooling and fringe, Hawk lifted one leg over the seat of the bike. He lifted the heavy machine with apparently little effort and settled it between his muscular thighs. She closed her eyes as her stomach shifted against itself. An image of his naked, sinewy flesh flashed in her mind. Her trepidation about riding behind him wasn't the only thing making her palms sweat.

She took a hesitant step forward.

"C'mon. Don't sweat it. I only live about three miles from here," he prompted. "Put the helmet on, and let's go."

"You'll go slow, right?" she squeaked as she slipped the black life-saving device over her hair.

His muffled reply never reached her ears as he kicked the very loud engine to full vigor. She climbed on behind him, found purchase for her feet and wrapped her arms around his leathered torso. Here we go. She closed her eyes as tightly as she could manage without making herself dizzy.

The bike's vibration shimmered through her as he turned them away from the building and onto the road. He slowly crawled toward the stop sign, then turned left and increased speed. Hopefully, the terrified squeal she released became lost in the roar of the engine and the howling wind.

She cracked her eyes open as her confidence increased. So far so good.

Suddenly, her own concerns scattered.

The images flashing past her tore at her soul. They had entered a residential section of the reservation apparently, and the condition of the homes amazed her. And not in a good way. Sad houses, mostly single wide trailers, sat haphazardly behind sagging chain link fences. A few of them boasted front porches, no more than stoops really, made from weather-damaged particleboard. The remaining tenants had stacked railroad ties or bricks to act as steps to the solid metal doors. Broken windows looked like crying eyes as the homes stared back at her.

Unhappy with the direction of her thoughts, she turned her head to face the other way. The opposite side of the street proved no better.

Hawk made another left, then a right before he slowed to a stop in front of a newer doublewide. He cut the engine and swung his leg over the bike in front of him, leaning his rear on the seat as he smiled in her direction.

"You can let go now." He laughed.

She hadn't realized she still clung fiercely to him until he pointed it out. She chuckled at herself as she let him go. Then she reached up and took off the helmet.

"That wasn't so bad, now was it?"

"I suppose not. You didn't kill me, anyway," she replied reluctantly.

"Let's go see what Jake made for dinner," he smirked as he pushed himself off the seat and helped her dismount.

He lifted his pack and her belongings from the saddlebags in one strong hand and escorted her to the front door. His free hand pressed against the small of her back and tendrils of heat bore through her.

Was she insane to spend the night here? Intelligent and worldly, she knew what would happen tonight. She doubted seriously if he intended her to sleep in a guest room. She answered her own silent question with a resounding "probably". But she didn't care. Her body already responded to the erotic thoughts running through her mind.

He opened the unlocked door and ushered her inside. The neatlyappointed living room into which she entered screamed, "Men live here!" Instead of a painting over the fireplace, an electronic dartboard hung over a collection of darts. The oversized sofa and twin chairs-and-a-halves looked comfortable and welcoming. The big, flat screen television nearly covered an entire wall as it tuned in a professional basketball game.

"Come on, you asshole! My grandmother could have made that lay-up," a man shouted from a battered recliner.

Candice jumped at the unexpected voice, placing a hand to her chest.

Hawk sighed and shook his head. "Candice, meet my brother Jake."

Chapter Eight

Hawk should have known better than to bring Candice to his place when the Timberwolves were playing. True to his usual form when the T-wolves played, he wore his team jersey, had painted his face in black and blue and gripped a reduced sized basketball with the wolf logo on it. Hawk sighed, retrieved a throw pillow from the end of the sofa and tossed it at the back of his brother's head.

"What the hell?" Jake turned and then laughed as he threw the pillow back. "Oh, it's you. Boozhoo, bro." He straightened to his full height as he eyed Candice. "And who do we have here?"

The strains of jealously coursing through him clawed at Hawk's gut like fire. He felt his expression narrow as he glared at his younger brother. He didn't like the feeling. He'd never been jealous of anyone. Ever confident and generally even-tempered, he'd prided himself for his realism and common sense. He ran a hand through his hair, willing his body to relax. This was the second time since he'd met Candice for the green-eyed beast to rear its scaled head.

The thought shook him as he set his pack and Candy's belongings on the sideboard by the front door.

"Candice Lincoln. She's staying with us tonight, so if you're having trouble with the T-wolves, I would suggest you turn off the game before you make a fool of yourself."

"Bite me, bro," Jake offered casually as he grabbed the remote and turned off the television. "Nice to meet you, Candice. Come on in and make yourself at home."

"Thanks, and you don't have to turn the game off for me. I have four brothers addicted to the NFL. I'm used to game day," she replied as she moved further into the room.

Hawk realized then he knew so little about her. Four brothers. This was the kind of personal information against the rules for a one-night stand. But then, so was having lunch, working together and spending the night together a second time. In his heart, Candice had left the realm of a casual-sex-one-nighter the moment he'd seen her. He knew it and it drove him to distraction. "What's for dinner?" Hawk's voice sounded clipped, even to himself.

Get a grip. Don't be an asshole.

"Navajo Tacos. I just have to fry the bread and we're set."

"Candy?" Hawk cleared his throat. "Make yourself comfortable. I'm going to help Shit-For-Brains in the kitchen for a sec and I'll be right back."

"Don't worry about me. I'm fine," she quipped, taking a seat on the sofa and pulling out her cell-phone charger from her satchel. "Um. Is there someplace I can plug this in?"

"Sure. Right behind that end table."

Jake pointed behind her.

Once in the kitchen, Hawk placed both his hands on the counter and lowered his head slightly.

"Man, where did you find her? She's hot." Jake's wolf whistle from behind him spun Hawk as swiftly as if he'd been punched.

"You keep your hands to yourself, you got me?"

Jake lifted both of his hands, palms out, in a posture of mock surrender. "Whoa, Gekek. Simmer down. I didn't mean anything by it."

Hawk groaned and turned away. He had no call to attack his own brother like that. What was happening to him? He felt like a starving man, his animal side lashing out in the most primitive of defenses. *Don't mess with my life's force.*

But Candice wasn't his life force.

Was she?

No. She's a one-night stand, that's all. So she'd soon be a double-header, but he would let her go after tonight. He didn't want the complications of a relationship right now.

"What's wrong with you?" Jake opened the refrigerator and pulled out several plastic containers of taco toppings.

I'm dying because I can't have her.

The whole thing seemed pretty ridiculous. His own honor and self prescribed mission to change the lives of his people stood guard over his heart like ancient warriors. He didn't have time for a personal life. And it seemed pretty unlikely a big-shot like Candice would either.

"Nothing, man. Sorry."

"You got something going with her?"

Hawk flipped the dial on the gas stove and moved a cast iron griddle over the blue flame. "Not really. It's just a fling, I guess."

He cast a sideways glance at Jake who didn't seem convinced.

"Whatever you say, Mike."

It's just a fling, I guess.

Hawk's words spun in her mind like a top. Candice nearly whimpered before she placed her hand over her mouth, turned on silent feet and walked back into the living room.

What did she think? He loved her?

She'd met him two days ago! And she certainly wasn't falling for him. She couldn't be. Their lives were too different, their cultures constantly clashing. The very thought of a relationship with him was...

Absurd.

So why did his words wound her to the pits of her soul?

"You okay in here?" Hawk crossed the living room and stood in relaxed composure as he leaned against a built in bookcase flanking the fireplace, smattered with snapshots, books and memorabilia.

"Yes," she lied.

"You want a drink?"

"Sure." I want champagne and strawberries.

"Coming right up. And dinner's almost ready."

His tall, straight back beckoned to her when he turned toward the small wet bar beside the television. Her fingers itched to take out his pony-tail and comb the long black strands. Her stomach clenched and liquid fire pooled in her gut. They would make love again tonight. It was unavoidable. She knew it as fact. Like air, water, food and shelter, touching him was necessary.

Almost frightened by the thought, she hugged herself with one hand across her midsection as she stood and took the drink he offered.

"You cold?" Hawk's eyes narrowed.

Freezing. "No, I'm fine."

Looking for something to take her mind off her childish fantasies, she stared at the photographs on the dark wood shelves. She found a picture of four men, three of them in full Native American regalia. Second from the left, Hawk's image smiled broadly, his hair braided with bright red and yellow feathers which matched the red, yellow and orange of the outfit. He looked like a mystical fire god. She also recognized Jake in the photo, his regalia more subtle, but if the patterns on the fabric were made of beads, as she suspected, it must have taken hundreds of hours to complete.

"Those are my other brothers," Hawk indicated. He appeared beside her, so close she could feel his body heat reaching out for her. She trembled inside. "That's me and Jake. And this is Remy, without the regalia, and that's Adam. He's a drummer. He also makes flutes and drums in the tradition of the old ways. They live in North Dakota."

"Do you see them much?"

"Every so often. Except for Adam. I see him all the time."

"He travels here, or do you go there?"

"He plays all the major Pow Wows. Since I usually dance at them, we keep tripping over each other." She liked the way his eyes lit up when he talked about his family. "He's also a dream-walker. Whenever something really, really important comes up, he might even show up in my dreams. It isn't often, but considering he's the oldest and feels sort of responsible for us, it happens."

Candice felt a cold shiver run up her spine. Born and raised in the real world, the concept of someone infiltrating another's dreams freaked her out just a little bit. Hawk must have sensed it as his muscles bunched and his body became as rigid as a board.

"Our father went to prison when we were all just kids. I was fourteen, and even though Adam was only sixteen, he sort of took over. Mom died when we were younger."

The ability to form a sentence escaped her. His father was in prison? She wanted to know why, how, but didn't ask. The memory obviously pained him.

"Soup's on, people," Jake yelled from the dining room.

Her tension dissipated somewhat with the normalcy of the statement. She squeaked, "Let's eat. I'm starving."

Throughout dinner, Jake kept the

conversation light and friendly. Candice found herself wondering about Hawk's childhood, how he managed to go to college with no mother and a father in prison. He could have so easily fallen into the trap of alcohol and despair like so many of his people. But instead, he'd focused his attention on changing the rules, making life better for himself and everyone around him. Amazed by his giving spirit, she wanted to know everything about him.

But she didn't ask the dozens of questions floating in her mind. She didn't have any right to.

After dinner, she insisted she help with the dishes. Jake ushered Hawk into the other room. "I know you brought work home with you. Go get it done. Candice and I can handle the kitchen."

Hawk left them alone, although Candice sensed he forced himself to.

Stop imagining things, little girl. It's just a fling. He said so himself. She pretended not to notice the stab of pain brought about by the thought.

"So what's your story?" Jake asked, his friendly tone softening the direct question.

She collected their plates and flatware and followed Jake into the kitchen. "I don't really have one," she sighed. "Raised in your typical middle class neighborhood in upstate New York. Constantly belabored by four overprotective brothers. Professional father, school teacher mother. College at University of Virginia, Charlottesville. Married the wrong guy, divorced the right guy and now I write for National

Pulse Magazine. The end."

"I doubt that."

"Really. There's nothing more to tell."

"You don't get to be a staff writer for a mag like the Pulse without some seriously hard work."

"You got that right. I worked my ass off for years. Covering news all over the world for a couple of other magazines and newspapers. Now I'm full time based in New York. It's steady work. I like it."

She lied and hoped he couldn't tell. He was easy to talk to and she feared she would spew out more information than she wanted Hawk to know. She had a feeling anything she told Jake, he would tell his brother. Not because he meant any harm, but because the brothers were obviously close.

"How long were you married?" Jake stacked the dishes she rinsed in the dishwasher.

"Four very miserable years."

"Marriage is rough, sometimes. I wouldn't know. I've never been married, and the only one of my brothers to give it shot is also divorced. I'm in no hurry, let me tell you."

Jake chuckled and then sighed. "Mike has always been too busy to find anyone. Man, that guy knew what he wanted when he was like twelve. Our dad always told us we could be whatever we wanted." Jake laughed at an apparently happy memory. "Mike took him seriously."

"How do you mean?" Candice tried to sound nonchalant, but the chance to learn more about the man working silently in the other room quickened her heart too much to let it go.

Jake wiped the counter and tossed the sponge into the sink. "You should know something about Mike, if what's going on here is what I think is going on. Mike is a workaholic. He spends every waking moment on the job. And when he's not working, he's practicing his dancing or performing at Pow Wow's to help keep the heritage alive and maybe even teach mainstream society that not all Indians are alchies and abusers. The kids around here listen to him, count on him, and follow him. Some of the adults hate him for trying the change things. A few of the elders are still bitter over our lost way of life. Attitudes like that sent the Nations into a downward spiral for years. Mike wanted to change the world. And now he is."

Any wild fantasies Candice had about falling in love with Hawk died painfully at Jake's words. She had no right to interfere with Hawk's life work. She wished she'd gone back to her hotel after all.

When she made love with him tonight, and there still remained no doubt in her mind that she would, she knew what small part of her heart he hadn't already taken would be his.

And she'd have to go home without it.

Chapter Nine

Hawk tried to concentrate on the financial files he'd brought home from the office. The government grants helped, but the reports were still a mess. He should be figuring out how to find more funds, but instead his mind kept returning to Candice.

Surrendering to his distraction, he closed the files and put them back in his pack. They could wait until morning. He poured himself another drink and ran a hand over his face. Tighter than a bowstring, his body throbbed with anticipation.

It was only seven-thirty. Too early for bed, unfortunately.

Already feeling guilty, he knew he'd have her tonight. He shouldn't. Not when he had no intention of offering her a commitment, or even a date. He shook his head at the dilemma. Leave her alone and let his heart wither into nothingness, or take her, feed from her, worship her while she was here, and let guilt kill him tomorrow.

Candice turned the corner into the living room and offered him a smile. Her lush curves called to him, making his shaft fill with blood like an injection. His painful erection cut into his jeans and he knew guilt would win. If he didn't do something, he'd throw her over the back of the sofa and take her right here.

He set his drink down and stared at her. "You feel like going for a walk?"

"Sure," she answered.

The sun wouldn't set for another couple of hours. The heat of the day had burned off, and even though a storm threatened, the wind had gentled to a low breeze as they stepped off the porch.

They walked in silence for about a half mile, before Hawk turned them toward an old barn with a dilapidated singlewide skeleton off to one side. "I just have to check on my horses," Hawk explained.

"Horses?"

"Of course. I'm an Indian. Don't you know all Indians have horses?" His lips spread into sexy, lop-sided grin.

She laughed at his joke. His ability to tease was one of the things she loved about him.

No. Not love. She erased the internal commentary with a swift stroke of her mental delete key. "Please... Native American," she teased back.

"Actually, I only have three left. I used to have about twenty head."

"What happened to them?"

"I sold them," he almost whispered.

"But you didn't want to?"

He shrugged his wide shoulders. He'd changed out of his work clothes and wore a black, chest hugging T-shirt and blue jeans with rough, worn holes in the knees. His hair hung loose around his shoulders now as well, and she shivered at the remembered feel of the silky strands caressing her breast as he made love to her.

"Some of the families here needed some things. More than I needed horses I rarely have time to ride, anyway."

He approached the fence and whistled loudly. A black horse with a white star in the center of his forehead dashed to the barbed wire and blew a loud greeting.

A smile rent his face, revealing his even white teeth. Her heart skipped a beat as she committed his expression to memory.

The horse leaned his head over the fence and Hawk pressed his forehead against the long snout, scratching behind the animal's ears with both hands.

If anyone had told Candice a week ago she would be completely relaxed in the middle of nowhere watching a man commune with a horse, not a single yellow cab or subway station in sight, she'd think they were crazy. But an image of making a home in a place like this suddenly appealed to her.

But only with Hawk.

Another piece of her heart jumped toward him and she winced.

She hoped he didn't notice.

"He's very beautiful," she spoke quietly, not wanting to interrupt, but needing to say something, anything, to get her mind off the impossible.

"He's a she. This is Blaze, that red one over there is Kennedy, the Appy belongs to Jake and there's a Pinto around here somewhere we call Warchild. Nobody rides him unless they want a battle on their hands."

His deep rich laughter filled her, making palms itch and his flesh tingle.

Lightning flashed and thunder vibrated the air around them with a loud, sudden crash. She jumped closer to him. Hawk's body heat reached out for her, soothing her like a favorite blanket.

"We better head back." He took her hand in his larger one.

Fire burned through her with more electrical current than any bolt of lightning.

By the time they reached the house, his arm encircled her shoulders and she leaned into him. She climbed the steps, surprised when he didn't follow, but turned her in his arms. Standing one step up from him, she still had to look up into his eyes, thought not so far as she normally did.

His smoldering black orbs examined her features as if he too wished to remember her face forever. She felt her blush suffuse her cheeks before she averted her gaze.

His fingers grazed her jaw, gently bringing her face back to his. Then his palm covered her cheek as his fingers imbedded in her hair.

"If you stay here tonight, I'll make love to you again."

He stated the fact plainly, the tilt of his head the only indication she needed to respond. It wasn't an invitation, but a warning.

"I know," she whispered.

"I don't want you to think badly of me, Candy. I have nothing to offer you." He moved his other hand to mirror the first, holding her head with gentle strength. He studied her lips and she willed him to taste them again.

"I know that, too."

He hesitated for only a second before he claimed her mouth with explosive passion. A moan escaped her throat as she felt herself leaning into his chest. He feasted on her lips before delving inside her mouth with his tongue, thrusting and teasing in a promise of things to come. Her whole body trembled against him with wanting. When one hand left her hair to cup her breast, her body responded with liquid fire low in her belly.

Her arms circled his neck and pulled him closer. She wanted to be inside him as badly as she wanted him inside her. He trailed his kiss away from her mouth and her head flew back of its own design. He nibbled her neck until his lips settled in the hollow of her throat.

He urged her from the steps to the porch and Candice didn't know how she'd managed to control her own movements without falling down. Her knees might as well be made of wax. Melting wax.

He broke off his attentions when he reached the door. Panting, he paused a moment before he opened it and led her inside.

Claiming her hand again, he dragged her inside behind him. The final quarter of the Timberwolves game shouted from the television while Jake threw a Dorito at the screen. He turned at their entrance.

Hawk pulled Candice behind him as he led her through the living room toward the bedroom hall. "We're going to bed, Jake. Knock on my door before eight a.m. and you die."

"Yeah, whatever. That's what I figured. You want me to turn down the tube?"

Hawk looked at Candice and allowed what he knew to be a wicked grin to spread across his face. Remembering her passion, he drolled, "No. You might want to turn it up."

He laughed at the adorable blush pinking Candice's cheeks. Her eyes widened to full moons.

"Way too much information, man," Jake responded as he used the remote to increase the volume of the game.

Hawk never broke stride as he led her to his room. The house had only two bedrooms, but they were both master suites, so he locked the door behind him, knowing they'd have no reason to leave before dawn. Except maybe a midnight kitchen raid. He had a feeling he'd need to keep his strength up.

For a moment, he did nothing but stare at her. More than beautiful, her features haunted him like some fey creature sent to torment and taunt. His jaw clenched as desire to hold her forever coursed through him. He pushed it way. He should be happy he had a chance to hold her again. And he was, for the moment. Even as the realization he couldn't keep her invaded his mind.

"Kiss me, Hawk," she called to him quietly.

He did. He renewed his attention on her full, pink lips, suckling until he felt them swell under his ministrations. Her chest rumbled with a soft groan, trembling against his diaphragm. He broke the kiss long enough to remove his T-shirt and toss it across the room. He dove on her neck, using his teeth to tease her hot flesh as he unbuttoned her top, slid it from her shoulders and let it fall to the floor, then used one hand to unhook her bra. He pulled one strap down with his hand and the other with his teeth. His loins swelled and pulsed, begging him to remove his jeans. He stopped kissing her and drew a ragged breath. Closing his eyes, he gritted his teeth. Sheer willpower the only thing preventing him from spilling in his pants.

She controlled his every thought. He belonged to her, and if she asked it of him, he'd spend the rest of his life worshiping her. She owned him.

Candice sat down on the edge of the bed, her full, naked breasts swaying gently with her movement. He reached for her, but she brushed his hand away.

Running her hands over his butt, she scooted him closer to her. He took a shaky step and gasped as her delicate fingers grazed his erection through his Levi's. She pulled open the top button and he groaned. He formed fists at his sides to keep himself from throwing her on the bed like some crazed beast.

She opened the second button on his 501's, her face so close to him he could feel her hot breath as it wove its way through his jeans. Finally, his member sprung free and she wrapped her hands around him. He thought he would die. *Please, don't let me die before she's finished.*

He leaned his head back, letting her explore him with her hands. When he felt the soft heat of her lips, and her humid heavy breath on him, he looked down to find her nipping lightly on his swollen shaft. She backed away and looked up at him with doe eyes and an evil smile.

"Oh god," he groaned through clenched teeth. "I can't stand it."

"You want me to stop?" she teased.

"No," he answered.

He watched her move her mouth closer to his shaft and kept his eyes trained on her as she swallowed him. He felt his climax growing in his groin, his stomach rumbled in anticipation. She moved her mouth slowly up and down his shaft, licking and nibbling until he thought he would explode inside her. She shoved her head forward, taking as much of his length as she could inside her throat.

He pushed her back then. "Stop," he groaned. "I can't take it anymore."

She grinned up at him as she laid down on her back. Her arms above her head, she stretched like a cat in a sunny window. He stretched beside her, taking her breast into his mouth as he worked the button and zipper on her jeans. Then he pulled the denim, and her lace panties, off together and settled his face between her legs.

"I owe you one, I think." He knew he smirked as what could only be described as anticipation crossed her face.

He ran one finger over her pink, wet flesh and almost hummed as the flower of her desire opened for him. He followed his finger with his lips and tongue. She writhed against him as he lapped at her center. He lifted her legs over his shoulders and her skin seared him.

"Omigod, Hawk. Don't stop. Oh god!" she screamed.

Her orgasm throbbed against his tongue and she tasted sweet, smelled of woman. Her juices dripped over his chin as she clenched her legs. Still he continued to worship her with his mouth. Only when she came a second time did he grant her new request that he stop.

He reached into his bedside table and removed a condom. Tearing it open with his teeth, he put it on with shaking hands. She opened her legs for him and welcomed him home with a heavy sigh.

Still wrapped in her descent to earth, she clung to him as he pushed himself inside her.

Warm. Tight. Home.

He moved his hips slowly, allowing her body to conform to his size. Letting her take the lead, he waited until her shifting pelvis begged him for more. Then he thrust inside her with mindless abandon, allowing her throbbing womb to take him over the edge.

He lost himself in the world existing only for them. If only the real world did not exist, he could stay with her forever.

She came around his shaft embedded deeply inside her, and whispered into his chest. The words muffled against him, but he heard them clearly enough.

"Love me, Hawk. Please love me."

The real world crashed around him.

Chapter Ten

Fear wrapped around Candice like a web. Would Hawk still be next to her if she opened her eyes? Inhaling the rich male scent of the pillow beneath her head, she forced her lids up and breathed a sigh of relief as she found Hawk staring at her. He laid on his side, his head propped in one hand.

"Good morning," he whispered, his voice rough with sleep.

"Good morning." She answered as she pushed herself up to mimic his position.

"I'd ask you how you slept, but I don't think either of us got much sleep. You are a wild-woman."

She released a nervous laugh. Only with him. She'd never done half the things she'd done with Hawk with anyone else. Not even her husband, and she'd considered their sex-life one of the good points of her failed marriage.

"I have to go to work." Hawk sighed, but made no move to leave the bed.

"So do I."

"You need to call a tow," he laughed. "And get a new rental car."

She laid her head into the crook of her arm as she remembered her out-ofcommission rental and groaned aloud. She needed to write her article and get it back to New York. She didn't have time to track down tow-trucks and deal with the red tape of a car-rental counter.

"But first, I think we should take a shower."

Her ears perked. Sliding gaze over the heated pools of his eyes, and then over the hard planes of his smooth, heavily muscled chest, she raised an eyebrow. "We?"

"Oh, absolutely. I'm big on water conservation."

She laughed again. Okay, so she didn't have time for this either. But she didn't care.

Two hours later, she climbed off Hawk's bike in front of his office building. Several young men stood over the open hood of her car. Instantly riled, she felt her temper flare.

"Hey, Mike. I think it's the starter."

The starter? They weren't trying to strip the car, they were trying to fix it. Shame clawed its way over her, pricking her flesh with knowledge she wasn't as cosmopolitan as she thought.

The boy in the middle waved to Hawk. She recognized him from yesterday. He was one of the young men Hawk had met with before they went to lunch.

"Thanks for looking at it for me, Jeremy," Hawk replied as he stowed his helmet and gathered his pack from the saddlebags.

"You asked him to fix my car?"

"Yeah. I called him last night. The kid's a whiz with anything under the hood."

"But I can't fix it. Don't have the parts. Sorry, Miss Lincoln."

"That's okay. I called a tow before we left Hawk's place."

"I have to get to work." Hawk faced her and took her into his arms.

"I know. Don't worry about me. I won't get in your way. I'll just wait out here for the truck."

He kissed her lightly on the tip of her nose. She inhaled the tangy scent of his leather jacket and smiled.

In a voice low enough the boys couldn't hear, he whispered, "Thanks for last night."

She didn't know what to say, except, "You're welcome."

You're welcome? She cringed inwardly.

"Can I see you later?"

Her heart stopped. The last thing she expected him to offer her was another chance to see him. Last night had been a bonus. Icing on a huge erotic cake. Could she risk seeing him again? Knowing he already held every piece of her heart and knowing she held none of his?

She didn't have a choice.

"Yes," she answered, the word in her head filled with hope and promise.

"Good. I'll cut out of here early and meet you at your hotel about eight?"

"Sounds good to me." Another night writhing in his arms sounded more than great.

"I hope you packed your glad rags, because I'm taking you dancing."

A real date? She nearly choked. This might be getting out of hand. But she couldn't resist smiling. "I'll be ready."

She watched his sauntering stride as he walked toward the doors of his office. He exchanged high-fives with the boys as he passed.

"He's a good guy, Miss Lincoln. Are you his girlfriend?"

Her attention snapped toward Jeremy Littlefeather. She didn't have an answer. Thankfully, the truck arrived and she didn't have to come up with one.

The boys said goodbye and meandered as a group toward the residential streets. She frowned as she wondered which of the houses she'd seen last night and again this morning housed the troubled young Jeremy.

"You need a ride back to the city?" The driver appeared friendly enough as he wiped his hands on a red cloth then tucked it back into the pocket of his coveralls.

"Yes, please."

Her bona-fide date with Hawk sprung into her mind. She had some shopping to do.

▲▼▲▼▲

"Michael?"

Hawk lifted his eyes from the computer screen and rubbed the ache from them with both hands. "Yeah, Celeste?"

"Mary Cadrieux is here to see you. She's pretty upset. Have you got a minute?"

"Sure, what's wrong?" He felt his brows close. Foreboding dread slithered up his spine.

"I'm not sure. But she's been crying."

"Send her in." Hawk moved the financial files off his desk and stood to meet Mary at the door.

A pretty girl of fifteen, she normally possessed the classic grace of her people. But when she came through the door, her shoulders slumped heavily and she hugged herself tightly around her waist.

"Mary?"

She raised red eyes toward him. Instead of speaking, she sobbed and ran toward him. He caught her in his arms as her momentum nearly knocked him over.

"What's wrong, baby?" His voice choked. He'd never seen her like this before.

"I'm sorry, Mike," she cried. "I didn't mean for it to happen. I didn't mean it. But he wouldn't listen to me. I tried to make him, but he wouldn't listen."

"Who, Mary? Make who do what?" Dear God, let him be wrong. Not Mary.

"I'm...," she began as he hiccuped a sob. "I'm pregnant."

Hawk's eyes fell closed as he held her tightly.

Fifteen. And pregnant.

He searched his memory for an image of who could have done this to her, but he couldn't remember ever seeing her with a boy.

"Who, Mary? I'll need to talk to him if I'm going to help you."

She stiffened. "No, you can't," she begged.

"I have to, Mary. This is serious."

"I know, but I already told him and

he doesn't care."

Bastard.

"Is he Native, or White?" At least he'd know where to concentrate his search. He would find the kid whether she liked it or not. Only question was, search the res, or search town.

"Mary? It's going to be alright. I'll help you. But you have to help me. You didn't do this by yourself. Now tell me."

"He's Ojibwe," she confessed into his chest.

Damn. He thought of his conversation with Jeremy Littlefeather yesterday. He'd come by to vent his frustrations concerning a girl. Jeremy wouldn't tell him which girl he talked about, but it had to be Mary. Jeremy was only sixteen.

"Jeremy," he voiced his suspicions.

She shook her head. "No, not him."

He pushed her away from his chest and bore his sympathetic eyes into her tearful one. "Mary. Tell me who," he demanded.

She withdrew for a hesitant moment before fresh tears cascaded over her streaked cheeks. "Justin Cross," she wailed.

Fury like he'd never known surged through him. He tightened his grip on her shoulders before he released her for fear of hurting her. Justin was twenty-four years old. This was more than horny kids not taking the right precautions; this was a crime.

He swallowed against the sick twisting in his stomach. "You wait here." He grabbed his jacket and keys and headed toward the door.

"Where are you going?"

Hawk stopped at the panic in her voice. "Don't worry about it. Just wait here. I'm going to have Celeste call your mother. If she gets here before I come back, tell her I'll stop by tonight and talk things over with her." He looked into the scared girl's face. "Your mother is good woman. It will be okay."

"Where are you going?" she repeated.

But he couldn't tell her. How could he explain he was going to find the man she probably fancied herself in love with and beat the holy, ever-loving shit out of him.

Hawk pushed the swinging door

away from him. He'd been in every dive bar in town until the odor of stale cigarettes and beer clung to him like a blanket.

The object of his fury sat at the bar with his back to the door. Justin hovered over his drink, grumbling to the white barkeep.

Without warning, Hawk grabbed Justin by the back of the shirt and threw him to the floor. Drunk, if the smell of whiskey on him indicated anything, Justin tried to gain his feet.

"Hey, Mike. What the hell are you doing?" Justin's words slurred as he stumbled to one knee.

"I'm kicking your ass, you pile of shit."

He clipped Justin's jaw with a right cross and sent the man flying backwards.

He dove on him then, driving his knees into Justin's stomach as he pummeled his face with closed fists.

"She's only fifteen, you bastard!"

Fury became a living part of him as he released years of pent up frustration at the plight of his people. The anger directed itself at Justin, but came from a much deeper place. Anger with himself for not changing things, for always trying and never making a damn bit of difference, fueled the fire in his fists. He was angry with Justin for taking advantage of a little girl, and furious with Mary for letting him.

With each fist landed on Justin's broken and bleeding face, he felt his control slipping further away.

"What the hell do you think you're doing, Mike?"

Rough hands grasped his arms and hauled him backwards. He snapped into reality at the sound of Carl Brandon's fierce bark. How long had he been beating on Justin? He looked at his knuckles and almost cried at the torn, bruised flesh.

Hawk sagged between the two men holding him fast. "I don't know."

"Four guys tried to get you off him before I got here," Carl knelt beside Justin's still form. "Damn it, Mike."

Hawk explained quickly, "He raped Mary."

"God." Carl stood and scratched his five o'clock shadow. He released a sigh before ushering them out of the way to allow the ambulance crew through the small crowd. "I'm sorry about that. But it doesn't give you the right..."

"I know, Carl."

"I hate to do this, Mike."

Hawk straightened to his full height. A shudder of shame and disbelief coursed through his pulsing bloodstream. Dear God, what had he done?

"Damn it." Carl took a set of shining silver handcuffs from his belt and turned Hawk around to face the bar. "Michael Manone Irontree, you have the right to remain silent. You have the right to an attorney..."

The words of the Miranda Rights drifted away. He had become everything he'd never wanted to be. He pictured his kids in his mind. Mary's tears. Jeremy's questions. Any number of good things he'd done in his life disappeared in this one act of rage.

How could he ever face them

again?

"Do you want to end up like your dad? Pure intentions are fine, Mike, but you can't take the law into your own hands. You know that as well as I do."

Carl's words cut him to the quick as he squeezed into the back of the patrol car. His eyes settled on the heavy metal barrier between himself and the front seat.

A cage.

Like an animal.

He closed his eyes for a moment, then forced himself to look at the truth. He deserved no solace. He'd acted of his own free will. He deserved whatever happened to him now.

As the jailhouse approached, he closed his eyes and saw only one face.

Candice.

Chapter Eleven

Candice looked at the clock and a flutter of excitement twisted in her belly. He'd be here in an hour. She laughed at herself as she examined her reflection. Wearing a little black mini-dress and new spiked heels, she put the finishing touches on her up-swept hair style.

Perfect make-up.

Fabulous Hair.

Sexy new dress.

She was as ready as she'd ever get.

She checked her watch. He'd be here in fifty-seven minutes.

Her cell-phone chimed from inside the new Prada bag she'd bought on impulse as she'd shopped for her dress and shoes.

"Lincoln, here."

"Miss Lincoln, it's Celeste."

Candice's stomach dropped to her knees. Something had to be wrong. "What is it, Celeste? Is Hawk alright?"

She hated motorcycles. The image of his broken and bleeding body sprawled across the highway flashed in front of her eyes.

"Eya'. Yeah. I mean, he's not hurt or anything. Well, he tried to call his brother, but he's not home, and he called me but I don't have any money."

"What's wrong, Celeste? Why does Hawk need money?"

Silence ensued as Candice waited for any response.

Finally, she heard a sigh. "He's in jail. His bail is five thousand dollars."

"Jail? What happened? Is he okay?"

"I can't really tell you that. I don't know exactly what happened. I'm worried about him, Miss Lincoln. He never does anything to get arrested for. He's a good boy."

Candice answered without hesitation. "I'm on my way, Celeste. Please, tell Hawk I'm coming. I'll be there as soon as I can."

She clicked off the phone and grabbed the keys to her new rental car. Jail? What happened? Why was he in jail instead of picking her up to go dancing?

She barely knew him. Maybe he wasn't the upstanding citizen she thought he was. Maybe he was a criminal and she was a fool.

She dismissed the imaginings as impossible. It must be a misunderstanding. She climbed behind the wheel and revved the engine to life.

It was a three-hour drive to the small town outside the reservation. She planned on making it in less than two.

▲▼▲▼▲

"Your bail has been posted." Carl unlocked the cell door.

Hawk sat on a metal cot covered in a drab green blanket, leaning his back against the wall and resting the back of his head against the hard, gray cinderblocks.

Celeste must have finally reached Jake. He couldn't wait to face his little brother. He looked forward to it almost as much as he looked forward to the lobotomy he direly needed.

He pushed himself off the cot and left the cell. "Carl, I'm sorry about this."

"You have a crystal clear record. Mitigating circumstances. I'll talk to the prosecutor and see what we can do."

"Thanks, man." Hawk reached out to shake Carl's hand before he opened the solid metal door which led to the lobby of the small jail. He'd been here many times, but always on the other side of the bars. He shook his head. "I'm sorry, anyway."

"Take care of yourself, Mike."

The door creaked open, but instead of meeting his brother's expected face, he saw Candice's concerned expression.

She looked amazing. Her long legs, accentuated by black, strappy high heeled shoes, revealed themselves in sheer black stockings beneath a sheath of black fabric. Her bare shoulders peeked from the thin straps of the low cut dress. But more than her physical appearance, her very presence comforted him. He hardened instantly.

"What are you doing here?"

"We had a date, remember?" She smiled through her obvious worry.

She took a step toward him.

His embarrassment moved down a notch as he opened his arms and accepted her embrace. One thing was missing from her expression. Nowhere in her eyes did he read judgment.

"What happened, Hawk?"

"What did you hear?"

"Nothing. For all I know you failed to pay a parking ticket. But considering I just maxed out a brand new credit card on your bail, I'm thinking it's more than that."

He cringed. She'd done that for him? Five grand was nothing to sneeze at.

"I'll pay you back."

"I don't care about that. I know you will. Now tell me what happened?"

"Later. Can we just get out of here? I have a stop to make, if that's okay?"

"Sure. Anything."

They left the jail together. When he draped his arm over her shoulder she gasped. "Hawk? What happened to your hands? Oh my God."

"Later, okay?"

He gave her directions to Mary's

house.

"Do you want me to go with you?"

"No. I won't be long. I just want to make sure Mary's okay."

Candice watched from the car as a young girl opened the front door of the trailer. Her face puffy from tears, she grimaced at Hawk. The sound of her voice echoed all the way to the car, but the words were lost in the night. Candice narrowed her eyes. A man appeared behind the girl and ushered her back into the house. Hawk spoke to the man for a few minutes and then he too moved back inside.

Hawk stalked back to her and climbed into car. He said nothing as he stared straight ahead.

"What happened?" she asked, not really expecting an answer. Who was she to him anyway? It wasn't as if she were entitled to an explanation.

"Earlier today, I tracked down the man who got that little girl pregnant."

Candice swallowed past the lump in her throat. "And?"

"I beat him unconscious."

The words sounded hollow. Whatever rage had driven him to attack the man responsible had been replaced with a dejected spirit and bitterness. The emotions shone through his moist, black eyes as he looked at her.

"Mary hates me, now. That man was her father. He's a little less bitter, but he's ashamed of what I did. I can't blame him. I'm ashamed of myself."

"She doesn't hate you, Hawk. She's probably just confused and hurting. Things will be better tomorrow."

"I used to believe that."

▲▼▲▼▲

Jake rushed through the front door, his face flushed and his breathing ragged. "Where is he?"

"He's asleep," Candice answered. "Please, don't wake him up?"

Jake ran a hand through his hair and sat anxiously on the edge of the chair next to hers. "I just got back and heard what happened. Christ, I should have been here."

"You didn't know. And even if you were here, what could you have done?"

"I know. I just can't believe he did something this stupid. Jesus."

Candice didn't know what to think. Was Jake concerned for his brother or not? She pulled her legs on the chair and hugged her knees to her chest.

"Stupid?" Hawk's voice came from behind her.

Candice turned in her chair and then stood. "It's late. You should get some more sleep."

"I'm fine. I can't sleep anymore. What time is it?"

"One a.m."

The phone rang, making Candice jump at the unexpected sound.

Hawk stepped toward the phone. "I got it, I have a feeling it's for me."

"Adam?" Jake asked.

"How much you wanna bet?" Hawk's smile relieved her. He sounded a bit more like himself. He checked the caller ID box and laughed as he picked up the telephone. "What a surprise, Adam.

And how are you this fine, very early morning?"

Hawk hid the sigh he felt like releasing. Time for the lecture and the cryptic warnings. Having a dream-walker for a brother had been a blessing and curse. Now was one of those curse moments.

"I'm fine. I have a feeling you've been better? What happened?"

Now Hawk did sigh, as he related a brief overview of the day's activities.

"I knew something was going to happen. But I don't think this is it. You still have a decision to make. But it's more than an instantaneous kind of thing, like kicking the crap out of someone. It's deeper and more life-changing than that."

Hawk threw a sidelong glance at Candice as she curled herself back into her chair. She fiddled with her fingers in her lap, staring absently down as she apparently granted him a moment of privacy.

"You know, bro, for me, getting arrested could be considered pretty damn life-changing. But I'm sure I can handle whatever it."

"So, when will you know if you're going to move in with Dad?"

Hawk rolled his eyes. "I'm sure it won't be that bad. I have friends in high places around here and that sonofabitch deserved what he got."

"Either way, keep me posted?"

"Of course, bro."

He hung up the phone and stood behind Candice's chair. He placed his hands on her shoulders and she rolled her head to one side. He needed to touch her. To know she was real and not some wishful thought. "You must be exhausted."

"A little."

"C'mon. I've got some sweats you can swim in."

She followed him to his room and sat on the edge of the bed. His gut clenched as her taste somehow filled his mouth. He wanted her again. He always wanted her. Ignoring the pulse in his groin, he grabbed a pair of sweatpants and a T-shirt from his dresser and handed them to her.

"What am I supposed to do with these?" She refused to take them.

He watched the desire play in her eyes. "Wear them. It'll be more comfortable than what you've got on."

Suddenly, he felt the veriest of all

scum. "Shit, Candy. I'm sorry. I ruined everything, didn't I? I didn't even tell you how amazing you look."

"No, you didn't," she pouted, pushing out her bottom lip. He wanted to sink his teeth into it so badly he thought he would choke on his own pride.

"You look amazing," he whispered instead, his mind suddenly blank. She stole his reasoning as easily as she did his heartbeat.

"Well, thank you very much." She smiled and turned her back on him. "Now that that's out of the way, would you mind helping me with my zipper?"

"Are you sure? I really thought you would have gone back to your hotel after you dropped me off."

"I'm sure, Hawk. I want to be here with you."

"I'm glad. Finding you here when I woke up was one of the best surprises in my life."

He slid the zipper down her back and she shucked out of the small dress. She wore a garter belt, thong panties and thigh high silk stockings. He groaned as he wrapped his arms around her and kissed her breathless.

Just one more time. He needed her just one more time.

Chapter Twelve

Candice didn't want to leave Minnesota. Her flight, scheduled to leave at six p.m., heralded an end to what had become a rich fantasy. She slipped out of Hawk's bed and padded to the bathroom. Her head turned to the sound of Mozart in digitized chimes.

She dashed to her purse and quickly answered before the annoying ring woke Hawk.

"Lincoln, here," she whispered as she slipped out the bedroom door and stood in the hallway wearing nothing but Hawk's borrowed T-shirt. Thankfully, it hung nearly to her knees.

"Why are you whispering?" The dragon's voice boomed in her ear.

She pulled the tiny phone away from her head and rolled her eyes. "I'm not whispering," she stated in her normal voice. "I had a frog in my throat. What's up, Mark?"

"Just checking your progress. I haven't received an email with your rough yet."

She cringed as she leaned against the hallway wall and lifted her eyes to the ceiling. "I ran into a snag. You'll have something before I get on the plane and I'll bring my photos with me to the office in the morning."

"What kind of snag?"

From Mark's tone of voice, she knew she skated on thin ice. All he needed was a reason to get rid of her. Her lack of ability to concentrate over the last couple of days hadn't exactly been helping her cause with the overbearing editor.

She thought for a moment, then decided the best lies have a smattering of truth. "The guy I'm working with, the hoop dancer, is also the Social Worker here on the reservation. Once of the girls he works with, a child really, has come up pregnant and he's been too busy to help much. But I have an appointment with him today at noon."

"The reservation social worker knocked up some kid," Mark's

astonished voice rang through her phone.

"No!" Candice replied sharply, then lowered her voice when she feared she'd awaken Hawk or Jake. "No. But it's his job to council her. God, Mark, you're sick, you know that?"

"Watch it, cupcake. So does that happen a lot? Teenage pregnancy, shit like that?"

"Yeah," she croaked. "The unemployment rate is sky high, the pregnancy rate for unmarried girls is a close second. And the houses these people live in, Mark. It breaks your heart."

Silence met her comments. She could hear Mark's breath on the other end of the line, but he said nothing. Could it be possible the man has a heart to break? She never would have believed it a week ago.

"I have an idea," Mark drawled. He sounded...

Sinister?

Dread shook through her mind. Nope. No heart.

"What?" Her stomach clenched. Afraid to hear his answer, she knew he'd tell her anyway.

"Why don't you stick around for a little while longer? You're visiting the reservation again today, you said? Take a cruise around and get some shots of the living conditions, talk to some of the natives about the messed up system, that sort of thing. I can see a serious in depth expose here."

The words of the store clerk she'd met Monday echoed through her mind.

You're going to write a nice article,

right?

"Mark, I can't do that. There really isn't a story here." She lied.

"Sure you can. Your article about the cotton candy rocked. If you can do that, you can do this."

She looked at the closed bedroom door beside her. No, she couldn't.

"I just don't think..."

Mark cut her off with a booming authority. "Listen, Lincoln. You write what you're assigned. That's how this thing works. If you want a job here when you hike your ass back to New York, you'll do the investigation and write the damn article. And I want it juicy. And I want to know why this social worker fellow isn't doing his goddamn job."

The hollow sound indicating an open phone line disappeared. She gripped the phone in the palm of her hand and stared at it.

An expose. Her heart thumbed painfully in her chest. Some words in her profession boded ill for the subject of an article, no matter what the topic. Expose was one of them. Another was 'investigation.' 'Juicy.' Mark had used all three of them. She groaned.

How could she possibly conduct an investigation into the management of the reservation social affairs and programs, and to focus the attention on the Director of Social Services? On Hawk?

She pushed off the wall and squared her shoulders. She didn't have a choice. She needed her job.

It's business. Not personal.

She stole into the bedroom and gathered her clothing before slipping back into the hallway and dressing as quickly as she could. She glanced repeated at Jake's door, praying he wouldn't come out. He didn't and she pulled the dress over her skimpy panties before shoving the stockings into her bag. Picking up her keys from the sideboard and snatching her shoes with two fingers hooked under the thin straps of leather, she left the house.

She felt like crying and laughing at the same time. Of course it was personal. It was Hawk's whole life.

▲▼▲▼▲

"Where are you?" Hawk's head pounded as Candice picked up her cell-phone.

He'd woken to find her gone and

felt...

Hell, he didn't know how he felt, except lonely. Of course, he'd done the same to her, but that was before he really knew her. Before she knew him. It was different now. Right?

"I'm sorry, Hawk," she cooed. "I called my boss and arranged for a couple of more days out here. Like a little vacation. Sort of. So I came back to my hotel for some clothes and my work stuff. I'm actually only about an hour from you right now, on my way back."

Relief coursed through him like blood. How badly he needed her right now amazed him. And terrified him. He'd never needed anyone before. He'd spent last night making love to her for what he thought would be last time, again. But the gods seemed to have something else planned, for once again, he had been spared the agony of saying goodbye.

He couldn't think of a single thing in his life he'd done to deserve the pure grace of this woman.

"Cool. So how long will be here?"

Did he sound needy? He hated people who clung and whimpered their way through life. Bootstraps. He preferred the 'pick-yourself-up-by-the-bootstraps' kind of people. The kind he used to be before he realized if he didn't' hold her soon, he'd die.

"As long as it takes."

"As long as what takes?"

She cleared her throat. "For me to relax. I've been working too hard lately. Spending time with you has shown me that."

He smiled. "I think we both work too hard. I have to work today, but how about I take tomorrow off and we see the sights?"

"Sure. It sounds nice."

"Is something wrong, you don't sound yourself?"

"I'm fine."

Hawk relaxed as he heard her smile through the phone. "I'm just tired. I'll hang out and wait for you to get off work. We can have a quiet night in, tonight."

"Sounds like a plan. I'm heading to the office now. I'll see you tonight."

Hawk placed the kitchen phone receiver back into the cradle and looked at his brother. Jake spooned a mouthful of Cap'n Crunch and lifted his eyebrows.

"Well?" he asked around the spoon.

"She went to get a few things, that's

all. She's coming back now."

"I have to go out of town again, so I'll probably miss her. Unless she's spending the night?"

"She probably will," Hawk answered. He knew she would. Even though he should really cut bait with her. He needed to focus all of his energy on fixing the lives of his people. Chasing after some white woman in a short skirt wasn't going to help anyone.

Making his way to his motorcycle to head into the office, several hours late, he knew he lied. Having Candice in his life did one person a world of good.

Me.

Candice pulled her car off the side

of the road and parked behind a large truck when she saw Hawk steer his motorcycle into his office parking lot. She hated lying to him. Assuming he'd want to take today off, however, she'd thought to buy herself an hour to shoot pictures around the res.

Turns out she hadn't needed to, since she now had the entire day to skulk around like the lowest form of tabloid journalist. She rested her head on the steering wheel as she watched Hawk's limber frame climb off the bike and saunter into his building. Even from this distance, more than fifty yards away, she could make out the sinewy flesh of his strong neck, the play of light in his black hair.

Or maybe she just remembered those things. Making love to him had become a necessary thing. She might have been lonely before she met him, but she hadn't been miserable. She knew without a doubt, the moment he read the article Mark forced her to write, he'd never speak to her again.

Much less, hold her in his arms and whisper, in his erotic, thick, native language, words meant to woo her heart. She closed her eyes when she no longer saw him.

If she couldn't see him, sight seemed pointless.

The deep breath she drew did nothing to soothe the hints of predicted regret strumming through her. She teetered on the edge of full blown deception and the dizziness from looking into the black abyss haunted her.

Her cell-phone rang out, shattering

the dismal illusion.

"Lincoln, here."

"I didn't get my check yesterday."

Of course he didn't. Fred, her ex-husband, only called her when he didn't get his check, or he'd heard she got a raise, or he wanted something from her, usually a romp in the sack.

"I have it on an automatic deduction. If it wasn't sent out, it's not my fault. I'll call accounting and find out what happened."

"You know, I put up with a lot of shit from you for a long time. I deserve that money. The judge said so. Fifteen hundred a month. Until I get married again or die. And I ain't getting married."

She didn't care if he got married again or not. In her present mood, she'd prefer the other option anyway. "I don't have time for this, Fred. I'm working."

She hung up the phone and tossed it into the passenger seat. Running a hand through her hair, she heaved a weary sigh.

With a promise of tears burning behind her eyes, she put the car in gear and drove to what could only be the beginning of the end.

Of Hawk.

Chapter Thirteen

Two hours later, Candice sat in her car. She'd taken four rolls of pictures and spoken to several residents. She'd seen the effects of alcoholism in the swollen features of several elders, she'd learned about child abuse from a young man in a wheel chair who'd been crippled by his own mother.

She also learned about love and patience from a young mother who despite the strikes against her, studied to become a nurse. She had seen kindness is the faces of three young girls who picked wildflowers while she photographed them and then crossed the field to give their collection to her. She'd seen hope in the faces of these people. Not laziness, and certainly not anything different than she would see in the faces of any other group of financially challenged people.

She loaded a new roll of film in her Nikon and focused out the driver's side window.

A knot of boys grouped together beside the sagging front porch of one of the rare site-built homes on the reservation. The clapboard house cried for a new roof, warped plywood covered one missing window and only a few boards retained their original white paint where the wind, sun and rain had stripped the pristine color away. Two of the boys straddled rusted bicycles, three leaned against the dilapidated porch and another four sat on the withering grass in the yard.

Jeremy Littlefeather wasn't among them, nor were the other two boys she'd seen with him. She could only hope none of these boys were especially friendly with Hawk.

Damn.

If she weren't careful, she'd lose herself in the lies. Pain ripped her soul as she realized it didn't matter if she did. She'd be lucky to look at herself in the mirror in a week.

She aimed her camera on the children and snapped several shots. Zooming in on their faces, each in turn, she photographed the whole scene. A girl stepped out of the front door with a toddler in front of her and an infant in her arms.

Candice snapped several shots of the girl, and her heart wrenched. She didn't look much older than sixteen. She gasped as the girl's eyes fell directly into the lens.

All of the boys noticed her then as well. Shame and fear crept over gooseflesh as three of them rose and walked her way.

"Hey you! What are you doing?" They called to her.

She took a breath, steadied her nerves and got out of the car. She could do this. She'd interviewed Saddam Hussein, for crying out loud. She could handle a few little boys.

"I'm just taking some photos, if that's okay?" She offered what she hoped was a friendly, open smile.

The boys appeared suspicious. She couldn't blame them, even as she kept that fake, misleading smile on her face. She was going to hell for this. No doubt about it. She'd sold her soul to the devil for her job, and when she wrote the article, she would cash the check.

"What for?"

"National Pulse Magazine."

"What's it about?"

"Well. It's about a lot of things. My editor wants to know what it's really like here. Are you happy? Are you discouraged? And maybe bring a little attention to any problems you have."

"What for? Nobody gives a shit about us. Especially white people." The boy in the middle raised an eyebrow in her direction. Handsome, he appeared older than the others by a year or two.

"Lonnie, what's she want?" The girl from the porch yelled as she tried to calm her infant, who'd begun to scream and squirm.

"She's a reporter," the same boy called back to her. "Wait a sec."

"Is that your family?"

He nodded sheepishly, as if he were embarrassed. "I'm Lonnie Cross, and that's my girlfriend, Beth. The boy there is Kenny, he's not mine. The baby is Elisabeth. She's three months old."

"You have a very nice family, Lonnie," she said. "You should be very proud."

"Proud? Lady, we used to be proud. A hundred years ago, maybe a little more, this was our land. We didn't use it with the blessing of the government and a few lousy hunks of cheese or spoiled beef. It was ours. You people came and took it, like you had the right or something. So do me a favor, and don't talk to me about pride."

The pain in Lonnie's eyes reached out to her. Hawk had his job cut out for him if he expected to change the attitudes of his people any time soon, if this boy's outburst, and the nodding assent of his friends, were any indication.

She didn't know what to say. She certainly hadn't run his forefather's off their land. She hadn't been born yet. Hell, her grandparents hadn't been born yet.

"I'm sorry that happened, Lonnie. Really, I am. But shouldn't you try to make the best of things now?"

He snorted. "How? Get a job in town, where more often than not some asshole throws stuff at me? No thanks. Me and mine, we'll stay right here."

"Lonnie," Beth crossed the yard and then the narrow street to where they stood beside Candice's car. "Just leave it alone. You don't have to talk to her if you don't want. I want to take a nap. Will you take the babies inside please?"

Lonnie took the baby from her arms and she watched his face light up. Bitter he may be, but he loved his child dearly. Would time and the challenges he faced erase the shimmering love from his eyes? Candice offered a quick, silent prayer they wouldn't.

Once Lonnie and his friends crossed the street, Candice focused her attention on the young girl in front of her.

Pretty, with straight black hair to her waist, she crossed her arms over her chest.

"You have to excuse him," she began. "He's been out of work for about a year now."

"How old are you?" Candice asked the question before she'd even known it formed in her mind.

Candice smiled. "I'm happy for you. Congratulations."

She should get in her car and leave. These were nice people and didn't deserve to be the subject of some bullshit article about how sad and poor they are.

"See, we almost lost Elisabeth. I was only a few weeks along and when I had to go to the hospital, Lonnie left his job to meet me there. His boss called him a worthless 'injun' and fired him that night.

He's been afraid to find a new job ever since."

"How do you live? Do you work?"

"No. Lonnie won't let me get a job. He says since I didn't finish school, the only thing I could do is waitress and he doesn't want some dirty white man grabbing at me."

"So, how do you live?" she repeated.

"We get our government money and stuff," Beth shrugged. "Welfare, AFDC. Food stamps."

Juice.

This is what Mark had hoped for. If a leading national news publication printed an article about the Native American community living off the federal dolls, the media frenzy would begin in earnest. Renewed debates on both sides of the issue would eventually sink the Native American population further into the annexes of history as lazy and worthless.

And Candice would be right there in the front, waving the battle banners.

"I have to go back, now." Beth's voice sounded tired, but not angry. She sighed, "Listen. I've seen your kind before. I know why you're here and what you're doing. Please don't use our names. Or the pictures, if you can help it. We have enough trouble with the townies thinking bad things about us, without adding something like this."

"I'll do my best, Beth."

Swallowing tears, Candice got back in her car and pointed it toward Hawk's house.

How could she face him? How

could she spend a 'quiet evening' with the man she loved, pretending she didn't twist a knife in his back? She couldn't do it.

After holding back her tears for most of the day, she finally relented. The tears poured over her cheeks, leaving heated chills in their wake.

She turned the car around and headed toward the highway.

▲▼▲▼▲

Hawk extinguished the tapered candle with his thumb and index finger, ignoring the singe of pain in the tips. He sunk back into the dining room chair and glanced at the clock.

Nine-thirty.

He'd called the hotel three times in

the last three hours. The desk clerk hadn't seen Candice since the morning. Candice either allowed her cell-phone battery to die, or she wasn't picking up.

"Hey, bro. What's going on," Jake said, flipping on the chandelier with the wall switch. "Why are you sitting here in the dark?"

"No reason," Hawk sighed.

A week ago, he'd been perfectly happy with his life. The kids on the res respected him, listened to him. Counted on him. He'd managed to completely erase all of that with one hot-headed, stupid act. His personal life lived happily in the background. He danced. It was all he needed.

He sure didn't feel like dancing now.

Without Candice, he had no reason

to dance. He had no reason to wake up tomorrow.

"Where is she, Mike?"

Hawk shrugged.

"Did she come by today?"

"I really don't want to talk about it," Hawk snapped, immediately feeling guilty for that as well. "I'm going to bed."

Once in his room, he laid down on the bed and stared at the ceiling. Her scent surrounded him, left on the sheets from the night before.

He reached for the phone beside his bed and dialed her cell number.

"Lincoln, here."

"Where are you, Candy? Are you okay?"

"I'm fine, Hawk," her sad voice replied. "I..."

Hawk listened to her sigh. His teeth

ached where they clenched tightly.

"I'm sorry, Hawk. I don't think we should see each other anymore."

"You want to tell me why?" Why did his chest hurt? Why couldn't he breathe?

"We're just different, Hawk. We live in different worlds, not just different states. It would have been better if we'd just left it alone after the weekend, you know?"

"Yeah, you're right," he lied. "No problem. Hey, I'll post my own money for the bail tomorrow. You won't have to worry about your credit card that way. Nice knowing you. Take care of yourself."

He hung up the phone.

Screw it.

He leaned back on his pillow and

pulled the opposite pillow, her pillow, over his face.

It smelled of her.

Whatever part of his heart still beat in the hollow cavity of his chest, beat only for Candice Lincoln.

Chapter Fourteen

"Boozhoo, Mike. How was dinner last night?"

Hawk didn't feel like talking, but Candice's little decision wasn't Celeste's fault. "She changed her plans."

"Oh, I'm sorry about that. I know you went to a lot of trouble. I sure do like her, Mike. She's a nice girl."

Too nice for him. His dirty little world had proved too much for her delicate nature, he guessed. As she pointed out, they lived in two different worlds. "Yeah, she's nice. Hey, can you call Mary's mother and set up an appointment for them to come in this afternoon? We need to arrange for a medical card for Mary as an emancipated teen so she can get her prenatal care set up through the clinic."

"Sure thing. Oh, and Deputy Brandon called about a half-hour ago. He wants you to call him back."

Hawk's spine tingled with trepidation. *Here we go. Time to pay up.* He set his pack on the imitation leather sofa in his office and ran a hand through his unbound hair. *What had the prosecutor decided? Would Hawk be charged with assault or attempted murder?*

He pinched the bridge of his nose between two fingers and sat on the edge of his desk. The phone loomed like a scorpion before him. Did he not reach for it, it would sting him anyway.

He grit his teeth and dialed the sheriff's office main number.

"Deputy Brandon, please," he told the female dispatcher who answered.

"He's on patrol. Is this Mike Irontree?"

"Yeah," he answered.

"Hi Mike, it's Carol Peltierre. Do you remember me?"

Carol had left the reservation four years ago. Discouraged with her chances here, she'd vowed to make it in the big city. He smiled. He knew she'd be back. She had always seemed to hold a special place in her heart for their traditions. Like him, she had found a balance between the two worlds. He cringed at the thought. Like he used to have. "Nice to have you back, Carol. I didn't know you worked for the sheriff's office. You're a dispatcher?"

"No way, Mike. I'm a cop. Just filling in for a while on the boards while I get to know everyone."

"That's great." He hoped the hollow ring in his voice didn't transmit over the phone line. He felt a surge of happiness for her. He should be thrilled she'd made so much of her life. A week ago he would have relished the fact that maybe, just maybe, he'd had some influence over her decisions and her success. It was his job, after all. But he didn't feel that way. He felt alone.

"Anyway, I can give Carl a message

for you, or have him call you later?"

"Whenever he gets the chance, Carol. I'm not going anywhere."

He hung up the phone and sat down behind his desk. The prospect of diving back into financial reports didn't exactly thrill him, either.

What had happened last night? He couldn't figure out what could possibly have changed between his phone conversation with Candice in the morning, and her failing to show up an hour later? Had she come by and then changed her mind? Or had he said something to frighten her away while they were on the phone?

He'd pushed too hard. That had to be it.

Damn it. He didn't mean to press her, but he'd never needed someone so badly. He silently railed at the fates for teasing him so mercilessly. Sure, he'd been able to leave her when he had the chance, but they kept throwing her in his face. Right up until the last second, when he couldn't breathe without her, then they snatched her away.

Figures.

A loud male voice rent through his closed office door. What could only be the sound of a fist crashing on the countertop in the lobby followed closely behind. Hawk jumped from his desk and dashed into the outer office.

"What's going on out here?" he snapped at Luke Champagne, an older Warrior who'd lived on the reservation his whole life, except the hellish two years he'd spent in Vietnam.

"I want to know why you would

bring some reporter here to make us look bad, Mike. That's what's going on."

"What are you talking about? Candice is writing about hoop dancing, Luke. She's harmless," he answered. Harmless to them, anyway.

"According to my daughter, Beth, she was poking around yesterday, asking Lonnie questions that had nothing to do with dancing. She took pictures of Beth and the babies. She better not publish them, that's all I have to say," Luke growled. "She better not use my daughter's face in some article about us. It's none of the white man's business what we do here. Or how we live our lives. They've done enough."

"Calm down, Luke. I'm sure it's a misunderstanding." It has to be.

"I'm not stupid, Mike. She may

have told you she wanted to write something on your dancing, but I'm tellin' you, she lied just to get access to the rest."

It couldn't be true. Candice wouldn't lie to him.

But she didn't show up yesterday. She blew him off like a mosquito on a summer night. As soon as she got the proverbial scoop she hunted for, she bailed.

The realization hit him like a fist. He'd been so afraid he'd used her, treated her badly. And the whole time, she'd played him like a drum.

He ran a trembling hand through his hair. "I'll get to the bottom of this, Luke. You know damn well I'd never do anything to hurt Beth."

Once Luke left the office, Hawk

turned to face Celeste.

"Hawk, I don't think you have all the facts. I can't believe that young woman would ever do anything like this. She seems so nice."

"Yeah, well, looks can be deceiving, Celeste. You should know that better than anyone." His gut clenched with sickening waves. "I'm going to see her."

"But..." Celeste stuttered.

He cut her off with one pointed finger as he went back to his office for his helmet and keys. "Do not call her. Do you hear me? Not one word to her."

He heard Celeste's sigh as he moved back through the office and pushed open the front door. "Fine, Mike. I won't call her. But I still don't believe it!"

Candice turned up the volume of her MP3 player as she developed the last of several rolls of film in her makeshift dark room at the hotel. The strains of Native American flutes she'd downloaded last night soothed her nerves, but not her conscience. As the image of Beth and her two small children appeared on the high quality photo stock, her stomach turned.

She was really going to do it.

She swallowed the surge of regret. She had no choice. If she wanted to keep her job, therefore allowing her to do little unnecessary things, like pay her rent, her alimony, buy food... She had no choice, she repeated.

Once this assignment ended, she

would no longer be reminded of Hawk, either. She'd spent nearly all of last night curled into a ball on the bed, hugging a pillow to her midsection. Intermittent regret mixed with tears born of loss as she'd avoided sleep. Exhausted, she'd risen early and written several paragraphs of her article.

"In the center of our pristine, pressed and starched, white collar world, lies the wreckage of a great Nation. Native Americans, Indians, live in squalor as government grants and other funds are used for ill-conceived social activities instead of education and community improvements. Pregnancy among the teen population of the Ojibwe Reservation in Minnesota rests precariously at 84 percent, while the unemployment rates rocket even higher.

Who feeds these children? Who tends the sick and the infirm? We do. American tax dollars feed the unwanted children, while their parents refuse to work, spending their government funded income on whiskey or other means to escape their beleaguered existence."

The words of her article tormented her. In her opinion, she'd written a work of fiction.

She believed none of it, but knew others would, regardless of whether any of it were true. She'd yet to send it to the Dragon. She hadn't been able to press "send" on the email program. Even as she developed the prints to go with the words, it sat in idle abandon on her laptop computer.

Her article concerning the magic of hoop dancing, where she'd expressed her amazement at the mystical power of the dance, the community and the man who shared it with her, rested under the surface of her desktop.

Taunting her.

The last picture developed, Candice stretched her back and rubbed her sore neck. She'd been stuck in the bathroom for hours, with only occasional breaks to hang the photos to dry in the main room.

She'd switched her music from the emotion filled beats of Native American drums and the mystery-laced flutes, to hard rock, which always numbed her. She still felt guilty as hell, but she'd been able to turn off her heart long enough to do what she had to do.

Now, she turned down the volume of Def Leppard's Pour Some Sugar On Me and reached for the doorknob. She immediately sensed she wasn't alone. A tremor of fear shivered up her spine.

Turning the corner into the bedroom area, she stopped short.

Hawk.

His back to her, he hadn't heard her approach. He held several crumpled photographs in his clenched fist as he...

Dear God. No.

Her knees weakened and her head swam with shame and regret.

As he read the screen of her computer.

Chapter Fifteen

"Oh my God," Candice whispered as she steadied herself against the wall with one hand. "What are you doing here?"

Hawk turned and glared at her. The pain and anger in his eyes burned through her like fire. No. More like spiky tendrils from hell itself.

"You really are doing this. I didn't believe them when they told me," he replied in a deadly, even tone.

"I..."

"Save it, Candice. Christ," he yelled. "I defended you! I told them they were wrong."

"I can explain. It's not me. It's my editor." She had to make him understand. She could take not being with him if she had to, but she couldn't accept his hate. Her palms broke into a sweat as she put the latest photos on the bed, not caring if they ruined.

"They are your words."

"But I don't want to write it. I have no choice." She rushed to him and placed her hands on his chest, her eyes lifted to his. Surely he could see how much she hurt for him?

His body became rigid, as if her touch repulsed him. He refused to look at her, focusing on something behind her, over her head.

"Please, Hawk. You have to believe me. I never wanted to hurt you."

"I don't believe you. I was so upset with myself about leaving you that first night. I thought you deserved better," he released a bitter, humorless laugh. "I must have been out of my mind. You used me. And I felt guilty about it."

He shifted his weight away from her and her hands fell into empty space. She felt so very alone, suddenly. As if the place where her heart had lived would never again be filled.

"Great pictures, by the way. You have a lot of talent," his words burned her anew.

"I'm sorry, Hawk."

He looked at her again, his eyes

narrowed into dangerous black dots. "My name is Michael. You have no right to call me by any other."

He was right, and she knew it. She'd lost that right when she'd turned on him. Regardless of the reason, a man of honor would never understand why she'd done it. Hell, she didn't even understand why. Not really.

A man who sold his own horses to provide for families not his own would never do such a horrible thing as she'd done. A man who risked his entire existence to punish someone for an act of cruelty would have made a different choice when it came to betraying someone close to him. She didn't deserve him.

He deserved better, and she told him so in a cracking voice.

The air in the hotel room thickened, even as the walls seemed to close in. Hawk inhaled deeply, but felt no satisfaction from the oxygen reaching his lungs. Dozens of photographs hung from strings around him. Pictures of his whole life. The people he'd dedicated his life to.

A stack of photos rested on the bedside table and he walked over to them. Using the fingers of one hand, he spread them out. His own image, dressed in regalia, danced from the glossy prints. These were the pictures she'd taken that first day. He lifted them with both hands and leafed through them.

She'd panicked when he'd teased her. She thought she'd captured his soul on film that day, thought she'd offended him. Well, she had his soul now. She should be pleased with herself.

"Why?" he asked without turning. He knew she still stood behind him. Her scent reached out to him. "That's all I really want to know. Why me?"

Her silence echoed in his mind and he turned to face her, holding up the photos. "Why me, Candice?"

"I don't know what you mean," she whimpered. She stared back at him with pleading eyes. But he was no man's fool. She'd tricked him once. He couldn't allow her to do it again. His people couldn't afford any more of her lies.

Her face and neck paled until he could make out the veins in her throat. The remembered heat of her skin beneath his teeth and lips seared through him.

"You knew who I was that first day. But did you really have to sleep with me? I mean, is that how you work? Did you sleep with everyone you've investigated for your little stories?"

"No," she answered, her temper showing in the pink of her cheeks as she moved from shock to fury. Her pleading expression changed to indignation in the span of one tortured heartbeat. "It's not like that. It's my job."

"You're job? Must be nice having that little line to fall back on."

"Stop it, Hawk. You don't know anything about me. You have no right to judge me."

He could feel her anger now. The six feet of tense air between them sizzled with it.

His own anger demanded release. And release it he would. He yelled, "I know everything I need to know. You use people. You manipulate. And you always get what you want. What else is there?"

"Get out. Get out and go back to your reservation and save your people. That's what you're good at right? Avoiding real life so you can play the worshiped hero? So go."

She marched to the door and threw it open. Her back straight, she stared at him. Fire shone in her blue eyes as her bangs fell in front of her face. He threw the photos on the bed and stalked past her as he muttered under his breath.

"I can't believe I fell in love with a woman who could this."

▲▼▲▼▲

Had she heard him right? Candice stood in stunned silence, her hand still gripping the doorknob painfully. The chime of the elevator had long since dissipated around her.

Hawk was gone. He'd said he loved her, and he was gone. Slowly, the crackle of her abandoned MP3 player ear-piece hanging around her neck invaded the silence, followed by the whisper of traffic from the city streets below her hotel balcony.

She shut the door and stumbled back into her room. The pictures she'd taken of Hawk while he danced strewn across the bedspread. Colorless and empty, they ridiculed her.

She looked at her laptop, the hideous article glared back at her. Trapped inside herself, the photographs and words of her betrayal ripped through her like claws. She wanted to scream. She wanted to pull her hair out.

She did neither.

Instead, she reached for the portable mouse and moved the cursor over the icon and clicked. Then she closed the lid and unplugged her accessories. She stoically packed the heavy computer into its case and began removing the pictures from the strings. She packed everything into a file and dumped them into her suitcase.

If she hurried, she could be packed and ready to go in a hour. Her flight didn't leave until tomorrow night, but she would get on standby now.

She couldn't stand to be in this room anymore. Her gut clenched as she remembered making love with Hawk on this very bed. Everything she looked at held a memory of him. The sliding glass door to her balcony caught her eye. The image of her back pressed against the cold glass as he'd driven himself into her, her legs wrapped around his lean waist, twisted inside of her. The television screamed at her as she recalled watching bits and pieces of "I Dream of Genie" while they'd eaten strawberries dipped in whipped cream, tasted champagne on each other's lips and intermittently explored each other's bodies.

How could she possibly forget him? How could she go back to New York City and pretend none of this ever happened?

She snapped her suitcase shut and slipped on her boots.

She'd just have to figure that out when she got there.

Because whatever chance she'd had to love Hawk had died the minute she'd allowed her idiot boss to dictate her life.

The minute she'd chosen to betray him, she might as well have severed her own jugular.

She'd made her bed, and now she had to lie in it.

Alone.

Chapter Sixteen

Three Months Later...

The airport hummed with the voices of strangers. The noise blurred in the back of Candice's mind as she waited for the last of the passengers to disembark Flight sixteen-forty two from London's Heathrow Airport.

Justin's dark head towered over the

other passengers as she spied him coming up the gangway. He smiled, throwing her a tired wave as he brushed past the crowd and headed straight for her.

"Hey, babe. Missed you," he chimed, sweeping her into a tight embrace. "The next time I tell you I want to go to war, remind me I'm gay, alright?"

She laughed. Barely recognizing the sound from her throat, she winced. She hadn't laughed in months. She thought she'd forgotten how.

At night, she laid awake, remembered passion filling her limbs until she ached for release. During the day, she worked quietly at her writing. Tired eyes focused on her friend now and she offered what couldn't be more than a wan smile.

"I'll do that, J. No problem."

"You look more tired than me, Candy. What gives. I didn't like the tone of your last email."

"I was probably just tired. Don't worry about it." She released his neck and stepped back. Changing the subject before she found herself in a puddle of tears in front of all of metropolitan New York, she quipped, "So is this everything, or do we need to stop by baggage claim?"

"Nope," Justin replied with a curious raise of his eyebrows. He patted his oversized backpack. "This is it. You didn't need to meet me. I can hail a cab by myself, you know."

How could she tell him she couldn't wait another minute to see him? She'd never been clingy in the past. But having Justin back, when the rest of her life rang hollow and empty, meant a return to some semblance of normalcy.

She sighed quietly as they made their way through the terminal. She could lie to herself with the best of them. Normalcy wasn't something she found these days, no matter how hard she looked.

They hailed a cab in front of the airport and Justin rang off their building address like a scripture reading. "I wanted to show you something, by the way," he drawled once the cab pulled away from the curb.

He reached his tanned hand into his pack and retrieved a battered magazine. Tapping the cover, he smiled. "This is the best damn article I've ever read, Candy. And I mean that. It's not just because I know you. I've never seen you write with such passion."

Her heart wrenched. She didn't think Justin had seen the piece she'd written. She almost hoped he hadn't. Wiping the sheen of sweat off her palms with the knees of her blue jeans, she stared out the window pretending to study the multicolored neon of New York's busy streets.

"Hey, babe. Look at me."

She obeyed, but only because not doing so would raise even more questions.

"I know what it must have taken out of you to write what you did. It can't have been easy."

"It wasn't. It was the hardest thing I've ever done."

"What happened to the hard ass Cotton Candy Whistle-blower? You look like you're going to cry." Justin opened his arms and pulled her trembling shoulders against his thickly muscled chest.

She sniffed back the silent tears threatening to escape her eyes. Just how many tears was a person born with, anyway? She'd expelled more than her share over the past several months. She should probably stop hoarding them, she sighed.

Justin rubbed her hair and placed a friendly kiss on the top of her head. "Have you told him how much you love him?"

"What," she gasped. Her head shot up and she stared at him.

"That Social Worker guy in your article. Have you told him how much he means to you?"

"How did you know?" Candice hadn't told Justin anything about Hawk. The wounds healed slowly and she still couldn't bring herself to talk about it with anyone. Not even Lynette had heard the full story.

"Come on, babe. I've been reading and critiquing your stuff since we were second years at UVA Charlottesville. You think I can't read between the lines? Nobody writes the kind of stuff you wrote and not love the person. Hell, I knew you loved him by the third paragraph.

Taken aback, Candice felt her eyes widen.

"Now the question is, since you obviously haven't told him, when do we leave for Minnesota?"

"Check," Hawk called to Lonnie, tossing him the basketball and waiting for him to throw it back. When he did, Hawk dribbled several times before passing to Jake, who went for the easy lay-up.

"Two points, and the crowd goes wild," he shouted.

Suddenly ransacked by the picture of a crumpled paper plate landing seamlessly in a trash can, he paused in mid stride.

Would he ever forget her?

"Hey, I've gotta jet. I'm going to be late for work as it is." Lonnie offered his closed fist to Hawk.

Hawk gently tapped the fist with his own and replied, "You better go then. Same time, same court tomorrow?"

"You bet." Lonnie trotted toward his small house, where Hawk could see Beth waiting with his lunchbox and car keys.

"He's come a long way, hasn't he?" Jake's voice swung Hawk around just in time to catch the regulation basketball his little brother tossed to him. "You up for some one on one? The rest of the guys cut out, too."

"Not really, bro." Hawk hadn't felt up to much of anything lately. The daily pick-up games started over a month ago, and he forced himself to play for the sake of the kids. He still tried to set a good example, mostly to redeem himself for attacking Jeremy Cross.

He followed Jake toward their bikes, parked side by side a few yards away.

At least that part of his life had worked out. When the prosecutor talked to the bartender, the white man had claimed he didn't see a thing, but remembered vividly Justin had been the only Native American in the bar that afternoon. And Justin Cross himself claimed to have fallen down the stairs. Everyone knew they lied. Carl Brandon had helped pull Hawk off an unconscious and bleeding Jeremy. But in the eyes of the law, with no witnesses willing to testify, and the prosecutor more interested in sending Justin away for statutory rape, no charges had been filed.

"Hi, Mike," Mary called from across the street. Her belly showed the beginning of a healthy pregnancy as she and Jeremy Littlefeather walked hand in hand on the uneven sidewalk.

"Hey, Mary. You taking care of yourself?"

"Yep. It's a girl. I found out yesterday."

"Congratulations. How's school?"

"Going good. I have a B in English," she stated proudly as they crossed the street toward him.

"Good job. I knew you could do it." With any luck, she still had a chance. She'd forgiven him for beating up Justin almost immediately. Since then, she'd enrolled in high school and become one of his most ardent volunteers.

"I think I want to be a writer."

A writer? Nothing could have prepared him for the impact of those words. Candice had certainly had an effect on everyone she'd met, and written about, since her time here.

But none more than him.

"Hey, you coming, man?" Jake revved the engine of his spider-theme custom Chopper.

"Yeah, I'm right behind you," Hawk answered as he climbed on his Indian. "I'll see you guys tomorrow. You're coming to the Pow Wow, right?"

"Wouldn't miss a chance to see you dance, man." Jeremy shook his hand before the two continued their walk.

He never knew when her image would haunt him, whose words would bring some terrible, gut-clenching memory to the surface. As he rode his bike down the same path he'd taken her, he could swear her arms encircled him.

He could still taste her.

He could still inhale her scent from his pillows.

He still loved her.

He turned the final corner to his house. A purple Mazda sat idle in the driveway beside Jake's Dodge. He parked in the street to keep from boxing in Jake's guest and climbed off the bike.

"I know you don't want to see me, but I couldn't stay away any more. I miss you."

It couldn't be.

He turned at the sound of Candice's voice. His heart lodged in his throat and he swallowed. Hard. Her hair piled on top of her head spilled haphazardly over her shoulders. Lips made for kissing twitched under his scrutiny. Eyes misted with unshed tears pleaded with him to listen.

How could he not? She looked like a glass of water to a man dying of thirst.

He craved her.

"I'm sorry for everything. I know I don't deserve you after what I did, but I had to try."

"I read your article."

"I wasn't sure if you'd seen it."

"Oh, trust me. Between Beth, Celeste, Jake, Jeremy and even Wiley Cotton, it was a bit hard to avoid."

Her eyes narrowed as she tilted her head, apparently confused by his statement.

"They each brought me a copy of Native Nations magazine as soon as it hit the stands."

"Wiley Cotton?" she stuttered.

"Yep. He came to apologize for every slur he'd ever spoken and asked if there was anything he could do to help. Lonnie's been working for him for almost three months, now, steady."

Candice bit her lip to prevent her tears from spilling. When she quit her job at National Pulse Magazine and refused to turn over her notes and photos, she had no idea the impact she would make on the people she'd met. She only knew she couldn't betray Hawk's love. Even if she never really got it back, she had to do the right thing in the ruins of her heart.

"Why didn't you publish the one you wrote first?"

"I couldn't do something like that. I hated myself for the pain I caused you, and your people. I was too ashamed."

"I'm glad you couldn't do it," he offered, taking a step toward her.

A slight quiver in her stomach told her to risk everything. The same force which told her to do the right thing three months ago. She listened, for the second time in her life.

"I love you, Michael Hawk Manone Irontree, and if you give me just one more chance, I swear," she choked back a sob. "I will do everything in my power to make you happy."

He opened his arms and smiled. "You already make me happy, ozawahn weenessisee."

She rushed to him, unable to conceive his ability to forgive and love. He took her lips in a deep kiss, his breath mingling with hers as he worshiped her with his mouth. Breathless, he pulled away and grinned.

"So you quit your job?"

"Uh-huh. I write freelance now. That's how the article about the spirit of your people got into Native Nation."

"So you can write from anywhere?"

"Pretty much. So long as I have my laptop and a modem. I'm golden."

"Can you write from bed? Because once we go through that door, I can't promise you when I'll let you go."

"Hawk," she chided him while her heart renewed itself with bursting joy. "You can't think of anything else that might occupy my time in your bed?"

The End

About the Author

Marjorie has been writing professionally for more than 10 years in various capacities and is an award-winning novelist. Nominated twice for the coveted Romantic Times Reviewers Choice Award for Best Romance from a Small Press, she currently resides in Utah with her wife and their shared eight natural, step, and elected children.

<u>Other Titles by Marjorie Jones</u>

Historical Romance
Writing as Marjorie Jones
The Jewel and the Sword (Medallion Press)
My Lady's Will (Champagne Books)
The Lighthorseman (Medallion Press)
The Flyer (Medallion Press)

Paranormal Romance
Writing as Starla Childs
Dawn of Love (Champagne Books)
Dawn of Redemption (Champagne Books)

Lesbian Fiction
Writing as Marjorie Jones
Hope (Indie Artist Press)
Loving the Heartland (Indie Artist Press)

Erotic Romance/Erotica
Writing as Raleigh Kincaid
Hunting Camion

LET INDIE ARTIST PRESS HELP YOU PUBLISH YOUR OWN COLLECTION OF POETRY OR OTHER BOOK!

Are you a writer? Looking to become an author through the art of publishing your novel, poetry, how-to book or memoir? If you've written a book and would like to learn more about the immense benefits of self-publishing, we'd like to help.

Indie Artist Press is the first non-publisher publisher dedicated to helping YOU succeed.

What makes us different from a vanity press?

A vanity press charges you for the privilege of printing/publishing your book. They do not:

- Edit your book for grammar or typing errors

- Edit your book for continuity
- Edit your book for characterization or plot
- Care, one way or another, whether you succeed
- Care, one way or another, whether they are selling quality literature

They don't care because you have already paid them! But that won't stop them from keeping 80% or more of each retail sale price, paying you only about 20% in royalties. You've paid the costs of publishing, and they keep the lion's share of your money. Sound fair? We didn't think so, either.

Indie Artist Press will charge you less and do so much more! **We can** :

- Edit your book for grammar, typing errors
- Edit your book for continuity,

characterization, plot

- Design a customized book cover
- Format your manuscript for print and digital distribution
- Help you set up your payee account through your bookseller of choice so that 100% of the proceeds of your book are delivered directly to you!
- Help you design your website and social marketing venues
- Create promotional materials to help you market your book
- Work with you to create a payment plan that fits your needs and overall goals for success

We have several plans to choose from, all for far less than you can expect to pay to a vanity press, or even a "traditional" publisher. When you "sell" your book to a publisher through a publishing contract, you are giving away up to 90% or more of your money for the rest of your life, and sometimes even longer. (When a publishing house contracts your book for the life of the copyright, that's your natural life, plus another 70 years.)

Why not invest in your own product by securing top-of-the-line editing and other services and then keep 100% of your earnings for the next several decades and beyond?

Please visit indieartistpress.com to learn more about how we can help you publish your first book, or your next book, with affordable, professional services.

Indie Artist Press